CHOICES

A NOVEL IN INTISH

CHOICES

A NOVEL IN INTISH

Noel David

Cover art by Park BC
In the conference room at Hidey High School (Chapter 2)

ISBN: 9781925555370

Trotwood Publishing
www.trotwoodpublishing.com
Sydney, Australia

First Edition.

DEDICATION

*To all those who want to or need to communicate in
English, and need the confidence to do so.*

ACKNOWLEDGMENTS

I wish to thank my friend David Kent for his encouragement and suggestions, and for allowing free access to material contained in his books *Intish: Introductory and International English* and *The Lyme Book*.

THE CHARACTERS

Staff at Hidey High School:

Ingrid MacElvers
Mark Kang
Maurice Hoare
Richard Tremayne
Peter Jenkins
Jon Mamjjasond

Neil Drummond
Betty Willis
Jenny Andrews
Jeff Bartrum
Patricia Williams
Tim Atherton

Students at Hidey High School:

YeongTae Kim

Hisham Moussa

Others in Sydney:

JinYeong Kim
SuHeui Ahn

Langton MacElvers
Omar Moussa

In Melbourne:

Andrea Mamjjasond
Joseph Mamjjasond
Margaret Mamjjasond

Barry Entwhistle (Brent)
Jody Greggs
Bev Morris

Others:

James Mamjjasond
Travis Nellow

Phillip (Skybee) Gray
Mary Gray

To encourage her students to talk more readily in her special English classes, **Ingrid MacElvers** choosed to speak with no exceptions to the basic rules when she beed at school, and gived her students choices to do the same. This novel be writed with no exceptions to the basic rules of English, but with most of the direct speech in standard English.

After a year, Ingrid's students haved to move on to regular classes, and **Maurice Hoare**, one of the grade eight English teachers, doedn't accept any difference from what he regarded as correct English.

YeongTae Kim hated English when he beed in Korea, but soon getted to enjoy it with Mrs. MacElvers. He beed back to hating it when he moved on to Mr. Hoare's class.

When the differences between Maurice and Ingrid becomed obvious, **Neil Drummond**, the vice principal of the school, seemed to have more sympathy for Maurice – until a serious situation developed with YeongTae.

Mark Kang beed YeongTae's mathematics teacher in grade eight, and he could understand him far more than he could understand Maurice.

Jon Mamjjasond beed one of Maurice's students fourteen years before, and he be yet another who doedn't like him. Jon goed on to become an English teacher himself, but he beed appointed to a school where he finded the students difficult to manage. With a wife and mother that beed also difficult, he decided to quit, but a chance encounter with YeongTae bringed him back to the classroom.

The story be setted in 1992 in Australia.

1

As Ingrid MacElvers beed looking at what her grade seven class handed in, Mark Kang knocked at the door and entered her office. "Neil wants to see you," he sayed.

"What about?" she asked.

"What do you think?"

"So Hoare and Tremayne have beed in his ear again."

"Apparently so."

"Mark, what do you think?"

"About your approach to teaching?"

"Yes."

"It's unusual, but I see nothing wrong with it. In fact, if I was teaching English, I would consider using that approach."

"Really?"

"Sure. What Hoare and Tremayne are doing is criminal as far as I can see, but then I'm only a mathematics teacher."

"Who need to use English."

"Well, yes, of course. What, are you suggesting that I speak the way that you do in my classes?"

"That be your choice, Mark."

"Exactly, which is more than you have at the moment. You better go and see Neil right now."

As they walked, they seed YeongTae Kim standing outside Maurice Hoare's classroom. "What are you doing out here?" Mark asked.

"I be standing, sir," YeongTae replied.

"What Mr. Kang mean be why you be standing out here," Ingrid sayed.

"I beed throwed out of his class again."

"Why?"

"Because I be refusing to speak the way that he be telling me to."

"YeongTae, would you like to come to my office?" Mark asked.

Just then, Maurice Hoare opened the classroom door. "What's going on here?" he demanded.

"I am asking YeongTae to come to my office."

"He stands there until the end of the period."

"If he be outside your classroom, he be no more long in your control," Ingrid remarked.

"That's true," Mark said. "Either you allow him back into your class, or he can choose to come to my office."

"Don't give Maurice any choices, Mark," Ingrid sayed. "As soon as we be goed, YeongTae will be out here again."

"What do you want to do, YeongTae?"

"I want to go to your office," YeongTae sayed.

The whole school must have heared Maurice Hoare close the door as he goed back to his class.

Even though Neil's door beed open, Ingrid knocked when she reached the vice principal's office. Neil Drummond lifted his eyes from what he beed writing and looked over the top of his glasses. "Come in, Ingrid. Oh, and please close the door."

She doed so. "What be the problem, Neil?"

"Please sit down."

"So what be the problem, Neil?" she repeated as she chose one of the two chairs on the opposite side of the large desk.

"That," Neil replied. "The way that you talk. Is that the way that you talk outside of the school?"

"It depend on who I be with."

Neil taked off his glasses and settled back in his chair. "Don't you think that, when you're with students who are sitting for exams where they need to use correct English, you should be setting an example?"

"Neil, don't you think that, with so many speakers of other languages that have arrived in Australia to live, we should acknowledge that we have at least two types of English in this country now?"

"Not really, Ingrid. You have informed me that schools around the world have English as one of their subjects. Now that would be either British English or American English, right?"

"Yes, right, but how many of those who have learned English as a second language can use what you regard as correct English every time that they open their mouths?"

"What do you regard as being correct English?"

"English where everyone can communicate effectively. So, I ask again: how many of those who have learned English as a second language can use what you regard as correct English every time that they open their mouths?"

"What do you think?"

"I really don't know, Neil. What I do know be that in every class that I have taked, if I insisted that students only used correct English every time that they speak or write, most of them would be afraid to speak, and they wouldn't write much."

"'What I do know be that in every class that I have taked.' Is that what you just said?"

"Yes, Neil, that be what I just sayed. Be there any part of it that you don't understand?"

"Ingrid, that's not the point."

"It be the point, Neil. What part of what I have sayed so far don't you understand?"

"Look, I've received complaints from …"

"You be not answering my question, Neil."

"Okay, fine. Of course I understand everything that you have said so far, but …"

"You have received complaints. From who? Any of my students?"

"No …"

"Their parents?"

"No …"

"Let me guess. Other teachers."

"Well, yes …"

"Let me guess again. Maurice Hoare and Richard Tremayne."

"Yes …"

"Anyone else?"

"The thing is …"

"Anyone else, Neil?"

"Ingrid, what you need to understand …"

"Yet again, Neil: anyone else?"

"Not that I know of."

"Probably because there be no one else. Look, Neil, some of the students that you have gived me have almost just stepped off the plane or ship, and within a year, all of them can read, write, speak, and listen well enough to understand every teacher and every other student in this school. True?"

"I think so."

"If you look at the records properly, you will know so. And then they move on to Maurice's and Richard's classes where anything that be different from standard English – the British standard – be counted as wrong and must be corrected, usually by writing the so-called correct form ten or twenty times for each so-called mistake. Now, be that okay with you, Neil?"

"If it gets them through their exams, yes."

"So you be saying that to pass any exam, each student's English have to be perfect? Be your English perfect, Neil?"

"Yes, I think so."

"Doedn't I hear you say the other day that our school reading program be very unique?"

"Yes. What's wrong with that?"

"Very unique, Neil? Either something be unique or it ben't. 'Unique' mean 'one of'. There be no degrees of 'one of'."

"All right, all right. I'm not doing exams anymore."

"Nor be I, but doedn't you say something about setting an example. Don't that apply to you as well?"

"Ingrid, the example that I'm setting is much closer to correct English than the example that you're setting."

"Which correct English, Neil? I assume that you mean the British standard. Why not the American standard?"

"That's fine."

"Then why be YeongTae Kim being told to write out sentences ten or twenty times when he use American spelling?"

"Well, we do use British spelling in Australia."

"And American. Whether or not you choose to vote for the Labor Party don't change the fact that there be no U in it. So I repeat: why be YeongTae Kim being told to write out sentences ten or twenty times when he use American spelling?"

"Why can't he stick with British spelling?"

"Because he never learned it. In Korea, he beed teached American spelling. YeongTae should not be telled to use British spelling, nor should he be sended out of the classroom for not speaking the English that Maurice Hoare require. What do you think, Neil?"

"Ingrid, I'm not about to comment on any teacher's teaching style."

"Then tell me why be I in here being questioned about my teaching style."

"I'm just following up on complaints."

"Okay, then, I wish to complain about the way that Maurice Hoare and Richard Tremayne ..."

"Put it in writing, Ingrid."

"I see. May I see what Maurice and Richard writed?"

"Ingrid, why do you encourage your students to use this simple English?"

"Be that what Maurice and Richard have writed?"

"Basically, yes."

"Basically. What else have they writed? Neil, I would really like to see it."

"I'm sorry, Ingrid, but ..."

"Then this conversation be over."

"Ingrid ..."

"For your information, I don't encourage any of my students to use a simple English. I offer them choices to speak and write with no exceptions to the basic rules. Hoare and Tremayne don't." Ingrid standed up and moved toward the door just as the bell ringed.

"Ingrid ..."

"I have a class now, Neil," she sayed as she opened the door. "I beed hoping to hand back the essays that they doed for homework." She leaved the door open as she walked out.

At the lunch break, Ingrid finded Mark in the staff room. "How did you go with Neil?" he asked.

"Not that well. How doed you go with YeongTae?"

"I'm not sure. I tried to get him to accept that Hoare will not change his ways, but ..."

"YeongTae want to keep fighting, right?"

"It seems that way."

"Well, good on him. It be pretty obvious that Neil will not do anything about Hoare and Tremayne, and that there ben't much that we can do."

"We could make a complaint, although it would be better if you did it."

"Complaints have to be in writing now."

"Were their complaints in writing?"

"I guess so. If they beed, I beedn't allowed to see them."

Just then, Maurice Hoare walked into the staff room and straight up to Mark. "How dare you take YeongTae Kim away from my class?" he shouted. "How bloody dare you? Don't you ever do that again! Do you hear me?"

"I think that the whole of Sydney can hear you," Ingrid remarked.

"This is not your concern, Ingrid. This is between Mark and I."

"Mark and I? Be that what you teach, Maurice? After a word like 'between', you use 'I' instead of 'me'? Maurice, you have some homework to do. Write out twenty times, 'This be between Mark and me.' And hand it in to me tomorrow morning before nine."

"Go to hell, Ingrid. You're in no position to tell me what to do and how to teach."

"I think that she is," Mark sayed. "You've made a complaint that Ingrid is not using correct English, and yet you have just said 'between you and I'. English isn't my first language, and yet I know that it's not correct English."

Maurice's hands suddenly closed tight and his face turned red. "Right, I'm going to give both of you fair warning. If either of you two ever go against me again in the way that I deal with students, there's going to be trouble."

"Another twenty lines, Maurice," Ingrid sayed. "Either of us be one person, so shouldn't you have sayed 'goes'?"

"Go to hell, Ingrid." Maurice headed toward the door, just as Neil Drummond beed about to enter.

"Let's go to the conference room," Neil said. "That's Ingrid, Maurice, and Mark."

"And Richard," Ingrid added.

"He can stay here. I see no need for him to be there."

"I can. He also maked a complaint about me."

"Fair enough. Richard?"

"I'm eating," Richard replied.

"Leave your card game and bring your lunch with you."

"I'm in the middle of a hand."

"I'm sure that someone can fill in for you."

In the conference room, Neil sitted at the head of table, with Maurice and Richard on his right, and Ingrid and Mark on his left. "There seems to be a problem here, and I want it sorted out as soon as possible."

"Seem," Ingrid remarked.

"I said 'seems', Ingrid."

"I be questioning the word, not the ending. You've beed well aware that there have beed a problem for some time."

"And what do you think that the problem is?"

"You know as well as I do, Neil. As well as everyone in this room including the gentleman – if I may use the term in a loose way – who have just telled me to go to hell – twice."

"That's not going to get us anywhere, Ingrid."

"Exactly – until he apologize."

"Apologize?" Maurice stared at Ingrid. "What drug are you on?"

Ingrid immediately standed up, turned, and headed to the door.

"Ingrid, we need you here," Neil sayed.

Ingrid turned back. "No, you don't. I be doing my job properly. My students and their parents be happy. That be until they move on to Maurice's and Richard's classes, and yet I be the one who beed questioned again this morning. I've haved enough of this, Neil ..."

"Ingrid ..."

"These two have no problem with sending students out their classes, which I doubt be legal, and yet, Neil, that seem to be okay with you. I have just telled you that this ... gentleman here have telled me to go to hell, and in front of you, he have sayed that I be on some kind of drug, which also seem to be okay with you. Neil, you know what the problem be, and it be obvious that my being here be preventing you from finding a solution." Ingrid turned and walked out, gently closing the door behind her.

For about ten seconds, the conference room beed in silence until Mark speaked. "She's right. The solution lies with you, Neil. She's doing wonders with her students, getting their enthusiasm, only to have it destroyed in some cases by you two." He looked at Maurice and Richard. "Look, I know what it's like to learn English as a second language. You are taught the structure and the exceptions; you do reading; you have to translate and do exercises to show that you understand; and it's boring. All through school, I hated English. Teachers would hit us whenever we made mistakes, and I don't see that sending kids out of the room is much better. You two focus on the structure of English way too much, putting your marks around every little difference from what you regard as correct English, and I've seen brilliant pieces of writing with green or purple all over them."

"Mark, don't you send kids out of the room?" Richard asked.

"Only for bad behavior – not for making mistakes."

"So if you have a student who doesn't do a maths problem in the way that you tell them to, what do you do?"

"I don't send him or her out of the room. Maybe he or she found another way of doing the problem and get the correct answer. Maurice, isn't YeongTae communicating effectively in English? Is there anything that he says or writes that you don't understand?"

"Mark, why don't you just stick with your mathematics?" Maurice replied.

"Right, I will." Mark rised up. "And I will tell the students in my home group to come and see me whenever they are thrown out of your class." He turned toward the door.

Neil speaked. "Mark …"

"You're right, Neil: there is a problem. And the solution is obvious." Mark beedn't quite as careful as Ingrid when he closed the door.

He haved hardly opened the staff room door when Ingrid rushed up to him. "Can we talk in private? Either your office or mine."

"Sure. Just let me get my lunch," he replied. As they walked to his office, "Are you okay?"

"Not exactly," she replied.

In his office, Mark locked the door, and they sitted down. "You're upset."

"I be extremely upsetted. I feel like walking out of the school right now and going back to Zimbabwe."

"Are you saying that things are better in Zimbabwe than they are here? That's not the impression that you've given me up until now. And what about your students? If you leave, who will take your classes? The way that Drummond is acting, it would probably be Hoare or Tremayne."

Ingrid breathed out heavily. "Yes, you be right, Mark. Do you know what I have finded with teaching? The more well that you do your job, the more that you suffer."

"I agree, but I doubt that it only applies to teaching."

"It probably don't."

There beed silence for several seconds before Mark spoke. "Ingrid, I think that what you are doing with your students is great, and I wish that I had teachers like you when I was learning English in school. Can I make a suggestion?"

"You want to give me some advice."

"How can I advise you when I don't know you that well? No, I just want to make a suggestion."

"I be listening, Mark."

"How about using the standard English when you're not teaching your students?"

"I do when I be outside the school."

"I mean inside the school."

"It be a good suggestion, and I have thinked about that. There be two reasons why I don't use standard English when I be in the school. First, I don't want to be switching to and from standard English while I be here, and I don't want any of my students to hear me using standard English outside the classroom. Second, I want to show other teachers how effective speaking and writing with no exceptions to the basic rules can be. What do you think, Mark?"

"They're good reasons, Ingrid. The only reason why I made the suggestion is to avoid trouble."

"You mean with Hoare, Tremayne, and now Drummond."

"Yes. Sorry. I know what you're going to say, and I withdraw the suggestion."

"Don't be sorry, Mark."

"No, you're right, Ingrid. Absolutely right, and I'm willing to support you in any way that I can."

"Thanks, Mark. I really appreciate it, but I be concerned that other students will pick on YeongTae because he have choosed not to move on to standard English."

"Oh, you don't need to worry about that. His character is as strong as yours."

"Yes, but what if the trouble become physical?"

"YeongTae will never start a fight, but he will finish it."

"He ben't exactly big for his age."

"Which gives him the advantage of speed. Ingrid, it's not the size of the man in the fight; it's the size of the fight in the man. I suppose that you know that his home life is not without its problems."

"Yes, I know. I wish that there be something that I can do for him."

"I don't see that there's anything. Anyway, I will have another quiet word with him about moving on to standard English. His brothers already have."

2

YeongTae's attempts to move on to standard English beed not noticed at first, resulting in more sets of ten or twenty lines for each 'mistake', but when Maurice suddenly realized, he stared at YeongTae. "Who has been talking to you?" he asked. "Let me guess. Mr. Kang. Am I right?"

"Yes, sir."

"I see. Well, you've missed a couple and I want those done as well. In fact, you can write them out forty times."

"Sir, the two that I missed be about spelling."

"Are about spelling. You can write out that sentence twenty times also."

"Sir, my spelling be – is not wrong. It is what I were teached in Korea."

"Was taught in Korea. That's another twenty lines."

"Yes, sir. Don't hold your breath."

"Excuse me?"

"I sayed, 'Don't hold your breath.' Be that another twenty lines?"

"That's another forty lines, and you can leave this room before you get any more. And stay outside the room where I can see you."

YeongTae rised from his table, stared at Maurice, and started to put his books into his bag.

"Leave your books there. You can get them later."

YeongTae throwed the last of his books into his bag, leaved the room, and kept walking.

Maurice rushed to the door. "Come back here!"

YeongTae finded Mark in front of the 8A class, and beed waved in and pointed to a spare seat. The work on the board beed what he teached to 8C more early that day. YeongTae getted his maths books out of his bag to continue with the exercises that would otherwise have beed homework.

Just then, Maurice appeared at the door, and opened it without knocking. "Come here!" he shouted at YeongTae.

"Excuse me for a moment," Mark sayed to his class and moved across to the door. "Let's go outside," he sayed to Maurice. "I assume that you just sent YeongTae out of your class."

"And I told him to stay where I can see him."

"And I've told him to come to me whenever you send him out of your class. As his home room teacher, my instruction takes priority. Now I suggest that you go back to your class, let me get on with my class, and that we talk about this later. Okay?"

"In front of Neil."

"And YeongTae."

After classes finished for the day, Neil taked his usual position at the head of the table in the conference room, with Peter Jenkins (the head of the English department), Maurice, and Richard to his right, and Ingrid, Mark, and YeongTae to his left. "This is the last time that I want to have a meeting on this issue," Neil started out, "so I want to arrive at a solution today."

"You know what the solution be," Ingrid sayed.

Mark putted his hand on her hand.

"I know very well what the solution is, Ingrid," Neil replied, "and you are choosing to ignore it."

Mark withdrawed his hand.

"What I be trying to ignore, Neil?" Ingrid asked. "Be you

telling me that there be something wrong with the way that I teach my classes?"

"And the stupid way that you speak," Maurice sayed.

"Maurice, I don't want to sound as if I be being personal here, but why don't you go and stick your head up the back end of a dead horse?"

"Ingrid, that remark is out of place," Neil sayed.

"Be that right? And being telled to go to hell ben't? Being asked what drug I be on ben't? ..."

"Ingrid ..."

"And now, being telled that the way that I speak ben't?"

"Ingrid ..."

"And suppose that you tell this meeting what be wrong with the way that I teach my classes. Let's hear it, Neil."

"Ingrid, we haven't got time for that."

"Oh, great! Maurice can make 'out of place' remarks without any comment, and when I say something that be not as 'out of place' ..."

"Ingrid!"

The room goed quiet.

Eventually, Mark speaked. "Neil, I don't want to tell you how to do your job, but we are not going to get to the solution if this meeting is going to continue like this. Ingrid's right: the solution doesn't lie with the way that she teaches or with the way that she talks. With all due respect, gentlemen," he looked at Maurice and Richard, "the solution lies with the way that you teach and the way that you discipline your students."

"What would you know about how to teach English?" Maurice asked.

"Maurice, I do teach in English."

"YeongTae, what happened today?" Neil asked.

"I be trying ..." YeongTae started.

"I am trying." Maurice sayed.

"Very trying," Ingrid remarked.

"Ingrid …" Neil started.

"See, here we go again, Neil. Maurice can say whatever he like, but as soon as I say something, you …"

"She be right!" YeongTae shouted. "Mrs. MacElvers and Mr. Kang be the most good teachers in this school. Mr. Hoare, you be the most bad, even more bad than any of the teachers that I haved in Korea. I have beed trying to get up to your standard …"

"No, you haven't," Maurice sayed.

"Let him finish," Peter sayed.

"I have beed trying to get up to your standard, and still you sended me out of the room today," YeongTae sayed.

"Neil, be it legal for a teacher to send students out the room?" Ingrid asked.

"It depends on the circumstances," Neil replied.

"As I understand it, the student need to be sended to someone with a note explaining what the circumstances be. Be I wrong on this?"

"Well, no, you're not wrong."

"So that lead me to wonder why I be being called to your office when I haven't sended any students out of the room during the time that I've beed here. Why be that, Neil?"

"Maurice, why did you send YeongTae out of the room today?"

"Without a note," Ingrid added.

"Because he didn't do all the work that I required."

"You wanted …" YeongTae started.

"Hang on, YeongTae," Peter sayed. "Can you be more specific?"

"Just that. He didn't do all the work that I required."

"What work?"

"The work that I required."

"Which is?"

"Maurice, what work did you require?" Neil asked.

After a pause, "Writing out his mistakes ten or twenty times."

"Twenty times," YeongTae sayed.

"And what be the nature of these mistakes?" Ingrid asked. "Differences from your standard of English?"

"Differences from the British standard," Maurice replied.

"Be that the same with you, Richard?"

Richard beed thinking about something else. "What?"

"Do you require your students to write out a sentence twenty times if there be a difference from the British standard?"

"It's usually ten times."

"Neil, don't you think that we have now arrived at the solution?"

"Before I answer that," Neil replied, "I still want to know what YeongTae didn't do that caused him to be sent out of the room today. Maurice?"

"I cannot remember exactly," Maurice replied.

"You cannot remember why you sended him out of the room!" Ingrid shouted. "Be you serious?"

"Ingrid …" Neil started.

"You cannot be serious, Maurice!"

"Ingrid …"

"Have I just sayed something that be out of place again, Neil? YeongTae, why doed Mr. Hoare send you out of his class today?"

"Because I doedn't write out what he sayed be spelling mistakes. I use American spelling because that what I beed teached in Korea, and it be what you accepted, Mrs. MacElvers."

"There you have it, Neil. Surely the solution be obvious to you by now. Whether it be or not, I don't see that Mark, YeongTae, and I need to remain here."

When she standed up, Mark and YeongTae doed the same, and they leaved together.

"She's right," Peter sayed after the door beed closed. "The solution does lie with us. More especially, with you two." He looked at Maurice and Richard.

"Peter, we're doing nothing wrong," Richard sayed. "We're required to bring students up to the standard of English that is required in Australia, and that's exactly what we're doing. Ingrid isn't."

"To be fair, Ingrid is teaching kids whose first language is not English, and she prefers to get them speaking and writing before they get up to the standard. Now if either of you gentlemen can tell me what's wrong with that approach, I'm all ears."

"Neil already knows," Maurice sayed.

"Well, I'm glad that he does, because I don't. Neil, why wasn't I told?"

"I thought that you already knew," Neil replied.

"Well I don't, do I? So my question still stands: what's wrong with Ingrid's approach?"

"Are you happy for her to go around the school speaking this simple English, and getting her students to speak and write it?" Maurice asked.

"Maurice, she's not getting her students to speak and write it; she's letting her students speak and write it. When they come to you, then they can be shown the standard English, and be encouraged to use it. Encouraged; not forced. Do you understand what I'm saying?"

Maurice and Richard looked at each other. "Not really," Richard sayed.

"All right, let me put it this way: no more lines, and no more sending students out of the class when you think that they've made mistakes. From now on, you can only send students out of class for discipline problems – to me with a note. Do you understand me now?"

"What I understand is that you're on Ingrid's side," Maurice sayed.

"I don't take sides. And why are we talking about sides? Ingrid is doing her job extremely well, and I'm asking you to work with her. Do either of you have a problem with that?"

There beed no response.

Neil standed up. "Let's assume that the silence means no, and that this meeting has achieved its purpose. Good day, gentlemen." As he goed into his office, Peter, Maurice, and Richard leaved the conference room without a word between them.

The next day, Maurice doedn't collect the lines that he setted the previous day. YeongTae beed disappointed: he havedn't doed them, and he beed ready for an argument. Instead, Maurice getted his classes to read a chapter of a novel, and just before the bell, he announced that the next day, he would read part of that chapter to the class for the students to write down.

That evening, YeongTae writed out the whole chapter, putting a line under each word that do not follow the basic rules of English. He beedn't bothered by words like 'better', 'further', and those that add 'er' or 'est' to the end, nor by words that don't add 's' or 'es' to show that there be more than one. There beed not many of those anyway. What doed bother him beed the words that don't add 'ed' to show what happened in the past, and add 's' or 'es' to show what happen in the present to some other person or thing. There beed a lot of those, and he beed also bothered by the different forms of 'be' which comed up a lot.

Nevertheless, he scored 19½ out of 20 the next day. It beed the top mark where few students scored above zero.

The day after that, Maurice announced that he beed giving the test again for a different part of the chapter, and that would be the mark that would count.

YeongTae immediately putted up his hand. "Must I do it, sir?"

"Of course. If you can do it once, you can do it again."

"That be not fair. I want to keep my 19½."

"You might get 20. You're doing the test again, Kim."

"No, sir."

"Excuse me?"

"No, sir."

"All right, don't do it again."

"Thank you, sir."

"You won't be thanking me when I give you zero."

YeongTae suddenly standed up and stared at Maurice. "What be your problem, sir? I doed what you asked for, I get the top mark, and you want to take it off me. Why?"

"Don't you talk to me like that, young man. You seem to have forgotten who's in charge of this class. Now sit down!"

YeongTae continued to stand and stare at Maurice.

"Didn't you hear me? Sit down! Sit down!!"

YeongTae doedn't move.

"Right, you can leave the room now!"

Just then, Peter Jenkins appeared at the door. "I think that you better come with me, YeongTae. Bring your bag."

YeongTae quickly throwed his books into his bag and marched to the door. "You be a waste of fresh air," he sayed to Maurice on his way out of the room.

"Let's go to my office," Peter sayed. They walked in

silence, and when they getted there, he opened the door, looked at YeongTae, and pointed to a chair. When they beed seated, "Now, YeongTae, suppose that you tell me what the shouting is about."

"Could you hear it, sir?"

"The whole neighborhood could hear it."

Peter remained quiet as YeongTae telled what happened.

"I see," he sayed when YeongTae finished. "Is there anything that you want to add?"

"No, sir."

"Okay. Just one more thing: what did you say to Mr. Hoare on your way out of the room?"

"I sayed that he be a waste of fresh air."

"I gather that you and Mr. Hoare don't get on well."

"Yes, sir."

"You do get on well?"

"No, sir."

"So you don't get on well."

"Yes, sir. I want to go back to Mrs. MacElvers's class."

"I'm afraid that is simply not possible, YeongTae."

"Why not, sir?"

"It's part of our school policy. You can have a year with her, and then you are required to move on to another teacher. In your case, that teacher is Mr. Hoare, so you need to go back to his class, apologize to him, and do that test again as he requires. So, can I trust you to go back to Mr. Hoare's classroom, apologize to him – and try to make it sound as though you mean it – and do the test again? Look, what's the big deal if the mark is lower than 19½?"

YeongTae sayed nothing.

"Now, for the rest of the year, you work toward speaking and writing in standard English, and have no more arguments in class. Okay? All right, stay here and think about it. There are a couple of things that I need to attend to. I'll be back before the end of the period, but if you decide to go back to the class before I get back, please close the door behind you."

Peter immediately goed to Maurice's classroom, knocked on the door, and opened it. "Have you got a minute?"

"Can't it wait?"

"Not really."

Maurice rolled his eyes and walked over to the door. "I was in the middle of a sentence, Peter."

"I apologize, but we need to talk about YeongTae."

"As you took him away from my class, he is no longer an issue for me."

"Let's talk outside."

"There's nothing to talk about."

"I think that there is."

"There's nothing, Peter."

"I see."

Peter almost haved his hand on the handle when the door to his office opened. "Not just yet, YeongTae."

YeongTae standed with his eyes opened wide.

"It seems that Mr. Hoare is not ready to let you back into his class just yet. Do you have any homework that you can do now? You can sit at my desk to do it, and if I'm not back by the end of this period, just let yourself out and go to your next class. Okay? Please don't leave this office before the bell goes."

YeongTae sat down and taked out his maths books, but instead of finding the area within two half-circles joined by two straight lines, he started to write a long note.

"I don't know what to do with him," Peter sayed in Neil's office. "He created an issue with YeongTae which was going out of control, and because I stepped in, he now wants nothing more to do with it."

Neil leaned back in his chair, and thinked for a few moments. "Peter, I cannot help thinking that he's still angry that you got the position of head of department and not him. What do you think?"

"After what I saw today, I'm absolutely convinced that you and the board made the right decision by not choosing him."

"You know, I'm just wondering if this school has carried him for too long."

"What do you mean?"

"I mean that maybe he would be more suited to another school."

"You mean: move him out? Where would he go? I mean: which school would accept him?"

"Good question." After a pause, "Mark tells me that Korea is always looking for native speakers of English."

"Korea?"

"What do you think?"

"Korea: where YeongTae Kim comes from."

Neil's eyes lighted up. "Yeah. Interesting, isn't it? If Maurice can shift the problem that he has created with a Korean onto us, maybe we can shift the problem that we have with Maurice to Korea."

"If he agrees to go there. I doubt that he will."

"I think that he will. I think that he's more suited to the teaching style there."

"Did Mark say that?"

"Mark doesn't know about this yet, so please don't say anything to him. I want to talk to him first."

"Of course. But maybe you should talk with Ingrid about Zimbabwe. I think that Maurice would fit in a lot better there."

"Yes. Yes, you could be right."

Just then, the bell ringed. When Peter returned to his office, he assumed that YeongTae haved goed to his next class.

YeongTae beed running home, and when he getted there, he beed relieved to find only the family dog. He quickly packed a bag, leaved the note on the kitchen table, and stroked the dog several times for what he hoped would be the last time. Out in the street, he looked around to see if anyone beed watching, brushed aside a tear, runned to a bank, and then to the nearby train station.

3

Outside of Sydney, YeongTae haved beed standing on the Hume Highway for quite a while, and he becomed worried that the first vehicle to stop would be a police car. When a small car doed stop at around three in the afternoon, he wasted no time with getting in.

"Where are you going?" the driver asked.

"Melbourne," YeongTae replied.

"Oh, that's wonderful. That's where I'm going, and I can use the company." As they started moving, "So what's in Melbourne?"

"What do you mean?"

"I mean: why are you going to Melbourne?"

"I have a friend there who can find me a job."

"Oh, right. What kind of job?"

"Anything."

"How old are you?"

"Sixteen."

"You don't look sixteen."

"I be Korean."

"Even for a Korean, you don't look sixteen. My best friend at school was Korean."

"Was."

"He was killed when he was riding his bike. A drunk driver hit him from behind. Anyway, what's your name"

"Franky Lee."

The driver looked at him for a couple of seconds. "What's your real name?"

"Franky Lee."

"Listen, mate, I don't speak Korean, but I do know that Franky is not a Korean name."

"It be my English name."

"Well, my only name is Jon Mamjjasond." After a while, "What are the fourth roots of 81?"

"What?"

"You must have done this in mathematics. What are the fourth roots of 81?"

"I don't remember."

"Work it out."

"To be honest, I've forgetted how to do that kind of thing."

"Find the square roots of the square roots of 81."

"The what?"

Jon pulled over to the side of the road and stopped. "When did you leave school?"

"Last year. I doedn't pass."

"Grade ten?"

"Yes."

"But you passed grade nine."

"Yes."

"Okay. What are the square roots of 81?"

"9."

"And?"

"9."

"Franky, or whatever your name is, if you passed grade nine maths, you would know that negative 9 is also a square root of 81. Look, I cannot take you any further because you are obviously not sixteen, and I don't want to get into trouble with the police. You're running away from home, right?"

YeongTae beed quiet.

"So you get to Melbourne and then what? If you have any friends there, what could they do for you? You have a problem at home, and you cannot live there. Is that it?"

"Yes."

"Then you need to see the police."

YeongTae's eyes opened wide.

"I'm serious. They're the only ones who can help to start with. Who else can help? Maybe your teachers, but you're not at school now, are you? Hang on, are you running away from school? You are, aren't you? Aren't you?"

"Yes."

"Bloody hell." Jon breathed out heavily. "Forget the police. They'll probably throw you into a cell for the night and take you back in the morning." He looked at YeongTae, breathed out heavily again, and started the engine.

"Where be we going?"

"There's no choice." Jon pulled out into the traffic, moved toward the center, and managed a U turn. "I'm taking you home. There's no way that I can leave you here."

"Ben't you going to Melbourne?"

"I'll get there eventually, YeongTae. Before you ask, I noticed the address label on your bag."

As they drove back into Sydney, YeongTae told what happened at the school without mentioning any names.

"You should have told your parents."

"No way. I would be in more bad trouble with them."

"You mean: worse trouble."

"Yes."

"I understand. YeongTae, do all Koreans who can speak English do it the way that you do?"

"No."

"Well, my Korean friend didn't. In fact, this is the first time that I've heard it. Which school is this? Is it Hidey High?"

"Yes. How doed you know?"

"That's my old high school. Is Mr. Kang still there?"

"Yes. Yes, he be."

"Mrs. Williams?"

"No."

"No, I guess not. She should be retired by now. How about Mr. Hoare?"

"He be there."

"And he's the one who's giving you the trouble, right?"

"Right."

"Nearly everyone hated him when I was there. In fact, I think that there is only one person in the school who didn't hate him."

"Who?"

"Maurice Bloody Hoare."

YeongTae smiled. "There be one other in the school now who seem to like him: another English teacher named Tremayne."

"I don't know him. Hoare … There are so many times that I wanted to punch his head in. I'm not embarrassed now to mention this, but at school, I was one of the more sensitive kids in the class. He was often late for class, and there is one time that I was being picked on by the other kids in the class, and I was crying when he turned up. That excuse for a teacher – a caring human being – told me that he was pleased to see that I was upset. Here's the best part: he told me to come back after school because I didn't write anything in class."

"Doed you?"

"I had to, or else my parents would have been informed. You're not the only one whose parents side with the teacher more than with their kids. We're nearly there. Down the next street?"

"The one after be more good."

Jon stopped the car in front of the house. "Do you want me to come with you?"

"I think that you should go."

"And leave you here? No way." Jon started the car again.

"What be you doing?"

"I'm moving up the street where we cannot be seen." Around the next corner, "Perhaps we should have gone to the police."

"I don't trust them."

"Why not?"

"I seed a police officer stop a car in the street and tell the driver that he beed using a mobile phone while he beed driving."

"Well, that is illegal. Good on him. He was doing his job."

"The driver insisted that he beedn't using a mobile."

"Well, what do you expect?"

"The driver also sayed that he doedn't have a mobile anywhere in the car, and asked the officer to search it. The officer refused. He sayed that he doedn't have to, and gived the driver a ticket. Then he turned to me, and telled me to disappear before he give me a ticket. So, I don't trust the police. No one around here trust the police."

"YeongTae, you cannot judge the police by just one officer. Come on, let's go and talk with them."

Just then, there beed a knock on the window on the passenger side of the car. "My brothers," YeongTae sayed. "I think that you should go," he sayed as he opened the door. "Thanks for your help." He getted out.

Jon getted out his side of the car, and as he walked around the front of the car to join YeongTae, he finded himself looking at two guys who beed much more tall than YeongTae and more tall than him. "What do you want?" one asked.

"I be okay," YeongTae sayed. "Please, you don't need to stay here."

"I'm not going anywhere," Jon sayed.

"Disappear," the other sayed. "If either of us see you again, you're history."

"I can handle this," YeongTae sayed. "There be no point for you to stay. Thanks again."

With two pairs of dark brown eyes almost burning through him, Jon backed away wanting to say something but not able to find the words. Maybe it beed time to visit his old high school.

In the school conference room the next morning, Neil Drummond beed in his usual place at the head of the table. To his right beed YeongTae and his parents, and to his left beed Mark Kang, Peter Jenkins, and Maurice Hoare. Whenever he could, YeongTae stared across the table at Maurice. At first, Maurice stared back, but beed soon avoiding YeongTae's eyes.

"I should introduce YeongTae's parents," Neil sayed. "This is his father JinYeong Kim and his mother SuHeui Ahn." Then he looked at YeongTae. "You have some explaining to do, young man. What the hell possessed you to leave the school, leave your home, and head out of Sydney? Well?"

"Ask him," YeongTae replied, pointing at Maurice.

"I'm asking you, YeongTae. You're extremely lucky that you weren't arrested. So, why did you leave the school, your home, and Sydney?"

"I leaved because of him." YeongTae again pointed at Maurice. "I getted the top mark in his stupid test, and because many others in the class doedn't get above zero, everyone have to do the test again, and my mark don't count."

"YeongTae, we talked about this yesterday," Peter sayed. "Didn't you agree that you should do it again and just accept whatever mark that you get?"

"No, sir. You sayed that be what I should do. I doedn't agree."

"I'm a little confused here," Mark sayed. "Maurice, why won't you accept the mark that YeongTae got the first time?"

"Because if he can do it once, he can do it again," Maurice replied.

"That doesn't answer my question. Why does he have to do it a second time?"

"Well, as I say, if he can do it once …"

"Maurice, are you saying that he copied?"

"I think that it's likely."

"Did you see him copying?" Neil asked.

"Well, no, but …"

"What mark did the person sitting next to him get?"

"I would have to check that."

"Just a minute," Mark sayed. As he translated, YeongTae's parents becomed angry, and JinYeong shouted at Maurice in Korean.

"That's an excellent question," Mark sayed. "Maurice, if YeongTae got the top mark, how can you say that he copied from someone else?"

"Well …" Maurice started. "He must've copied some of it."

"I never copy," YeongTae sayed. "Never. Everything that I do be my own. I be honest, Mr. Hoare, and I hate persons who ben't honest. I hate you, Mr. Hoare."

"YeongTae …" Neil started.

"I hate you! You can go straight to hell and take your stupid test with you."

"Enough, YeongTae! You've made your point. Mr. Kang, could you …?"

"Certainly," Mark replied, and again translated.

SuHeui then asked a question.

"She wants to know if YeongTae can go back to Ingrid's class."

"I've already explained that to YeongTae," Peter sayed.

"And?"

"Students who need to go into Ingrid's classes can stay there for one year at the most, then they must move on to regular classes."

"Could we make an exception for YeongTae?"

"Well, I guess that we could …"

"No," Neil sayed. "No exceptions."

"Why not?" Mark asked. "Don't you think that it's justified?"

"Once we make an exception for YeongTae, we would have to make more exceptions – probably to the point where all of Ingrid's grade seven students stay with her in grade eight as well, and that of course would give her too many students. Maurice, I'm giving you an instruction: no more lines for what you see as mistakes; you accept American spelling; no more sending students out of the classroom unless it's with a note to see either Peter or myself; and you are to accept YeongTae's 19½ that he achieved on the test. YeongTae, you are required to work toward standard English not only with Mr. Hoare but in all of your classes. Mark?"

When Mark finished translating, Mr. Kim looked at his son. "Okay?"

"Okay," YeongTae replied.

Mrs. Ahn smiled.

"They're happy," Mark sayed.

"Good," Neil sayed. "So on that note, this meeting is over. Thank you all for coming." He goed into his office.

Jon beed sitting outside the conference room and he standed when the others comed out.

"Oh, look who's here," Maurice sayed. "What brings you here, Mamjacent?"

"Nothing to concern you, Hoare," Jon replied.

"It's Mr. Hoare to you."

"And it's Mr. Mamjjasond to you."

"This is Jon Mamjjasond," Mark sayed. "He was here ..."

"1977 to 1982."

"Well, there have been a few changes in the last ten years. This is Peter Jenkins who has taken over from Patricia Williams, and this is YeongTae Kim and his parents."

"I think that you should also introduce Jon to the vice principal," Peter sayed.

"I was about to do that. Could you please excuse us?"

"Have you got a minute, Neil?" Mark asked. "This is Jon Mamjjasond who was here between 1977 and 1982."

"Well, it's nice that a few former students come back to see us every now and then. I'm Neil Drummond. I take it that Maurice Hoare took you for English in one of those years."

"Yes, sir."

"And that he isn't high on your list of favorite teachers."

"He doesn't appear anywhere on my list of favorite teachers."

"Well after hearing your little exchange out there, I'm not surprised. Why did you quit teaching?"

"Sir?"

"When you graduated from university, you went to teachers college and then to Kurropnagroopna. It's on your file with the department, and therefore it's on your file here which I just checked. You quit at the end of last year. Why?"

"I found that I couldn't work with students who have more rights than I ever had in school, and less responsibilities than I ever had in school."

"What are you doing now?" Mark asked.

"I'm still looking for a job. There are not a lot of opportunities for graduates in history and social sciences – except in teaching."

"Are you married?"

"I'm separated. Why do you ask?"

"Because it could be easy for you to get a job in Korea."

"Do you have kids?" Neil asked.

"None – not on my side anyway."

"I assume that you separated completely?"

"Completely. I had nothing, and she got half of that."

"Jon, I have contacts in Korea," Mark sayed. "I can get you a job in Korea if you want one."

"Doing what?"

"Teaching English. Actually, it's more like helping to further speaking and listening. Anyway, think about it and get back to me."

"Thank you, Mr. Kang."

"You can now call me Mark."

"Thank you, Mark. I certainly will get back to you – soon." Jon standed up.

"Jon, what did you come to see Mark about?" Neil asked.

"It's about YeongTae Kim."

"Really. How long have you known him?"

"About 19 hours. I'm the one who picked him up on the highway."

"I see. Where did he want to go?"

"Melbourne. I thought that I had some company until I realized that he isn't 16."

"Did he tell you that he's 16?"

"Yes."

"So much for always being honest."

"Sir?"

"He said at the meeting that he is always honest."

"He was honest with me once we got past this age thing. I suppose that you know that his home life isn't good."

"Yes, we do, but there's nothing that we can do about it until there's some real evidence of physical or emotional abuse. Then we would have to contact the police."

"Jon, I need to give you a bit of advice," Mark sayed. "If anyone in YeongTae's family finds out that you're the one who picked him up yesterday, I think that you would not be able to travel to Korea within the following few weeks. What I'm saying is that it's not a good idea to contact YeongTae again. And I don't know if I should say this, but I'm going to say it anyway. I don't think that it's wise to be picking up people from the side of the road – especially young boys. Can you understand why I'm saying this?"

"Yes. Yes, I can," Jon replied.

"And if I may add to the advice," Neil sayed, "the next time that you see Maurice Hoare, just ignore him – whatever he says. You're welcome to visit us again, and it's possible that we may need to see you again in regard to YeongTae."

"Sure." Jon then gave his phone number and leaved.

"Just before you go, Mark, how do you think that Maurice would go in Korea?"

"Teaching English?" Mark asked. "Neil, East Asian countries need first-language speakers of English who encourage speaking and listening. They don't get that in the schools because, in Korea at least, the high school graduate exam doesn't have it. And whether Maurice follows your instructions or not, there is no way that I would recommend him to anyone in Korea. I value my contacts there."

"So you don't want to help him."

"In a word: no."

"Mark, I could be looking for a way of getting him out of this school."

"Yes, I can understand that, Neil, but I have absolutely no interest in helping him. If he wants to go to Korea, he can do it himself." Mark standed up. "Neil, I'm not trying to tell you what you should do …"

"Then don't."

"Okay, fine." Mark turned toward the door.

"Do you have a suggestion, Mark?"

Mark turned back again. "Neil, Ingrid has told me more than once that she wants to transfer out of this school because she sees that you are giving her a hard time and going soft on Maurice and Richard."

"Mark, I need to …"

"What I'm suggesting is that you let Ingrid do her job, and give Maurice and Richard a hard time if they don't follow your instructions."

4

Even though he haved called ahead to say that there beed a serious matter that needed his attention, Jon beed worried about the likely reception in Melbourne as he drived out of Sydney along the same road that he beed on two days before. The warm sun and the clear sky beed promising a beautiful weekend – too good to waste on a trip to Melbourne for some family matter.

Soon after the road becomed limited access, he seed someone walking on the side. Despite Mark's advice, Jon stopped, and a tall, thin guy wearing tight clothes getted in, putted his bag between his foots, and smiled. "Tell me that you're going to Melbourne."

"Okay, I'm going to Melbourne," Jon replied.

"Oh, sweet. My name is Brent." He offered his hand.

Jon taked it, and beed surprised by its strength. "Jon."

Another smile. "Oh, don't worry. I've surprised quite a few people over the years. So let me guess: you live in Sydney."

"You looked at the license plate. Sydney isn't the only place in New South Wales."

"I know that, dear, but more people live in Sydney than in the rest of New South Wales, so is my guess correct?"

"Yes, it is. What about you? Do you live in Melbourne or Sydney?"

"Yes."

"Yes, what?"

"Melbourne or Sydney. Now it's your turn to guess."

"Oh, okay. Before I do, what football team do you follow?"

"I don't follow any football team. I hated football from when I was young, especially as I had to play it every winter in primary school and the first two years of high school."

"Why did you hate football?"

"I still do. Because I got hit far too often behind the play."

"That's part of the game."

"Not to the degree that I got hit. And of course, if I hit back, I was the one who was sent off the ground."

"Isn't that what you wanted?"

"Except that I would be put on report for a week, and that my parents would be told."

"Brent, perhaps I shouldn't ask …"

"Ask me anything, Jon."

"Are you …?"

"Yes, I'm gay. Always have been; always will be. Now, if you don't feel comfortable with that, you can stop the car and let me out."

"You'd get picked up by the police. No, let's go to Melbourne together. I've had a few friends who are gay."

"Had."

"Yes. All my friends from school have fallen out of touch. Isn't that the same for you?"

"I never had any friends at school."

"That's tough. Brent, can I ask how old you are?"

"Certainly."

Jon gived off half a laugh. "Brent, how old are you?"

"How old do you think I am?"

"In your thirties?"

"No."

"Twenties?"

"I'm 42."

"Really. Don't you mean 24?"

"I'm 42. Maybe you are 24."

"I'm 28."

There beed silence again for a while before Brent speaked.

"Are you married, Jon?"

"I was."

"Everything about you is in the past: you had friends from school; you were married. Let me guess: you had a job and now you don't."

"Correct."

"And you don't have kids. What do you have?"

"I have my health and my freedom. Isn't that the same for you?"

"Oh, that's so true. And I have a job."

"Doing what?"

"I manage a record store. Before you ask, I've just got back from America."

"You traveled abroad with that small pack?"

"Sure."

"Let me guess: you stayed the whole time in San Francisco."

"Oh, you're cute."

"But am I right?"

"No, you're not. I was more interested in natural scenes than the gay scene. I cannot live in America, so why look for a relationship there? Anyway, what happened to your relationship?"

"In a word: religion."

"Oh, let me guess. She's religious, and she promised that her beliefs would not affect the marriage."

"You're right."

"But you had to marry in a church, right?"

"Right."

"And within days of being married, the bit about her

religious beliefs not affecting the marriage went straight out the window. Am I right, or am I right?"

"You're right, Brent. Perhaps you should write a book about it."

"This story is so common that no one would read it. Listen, I'm sorry that your marriage went the way that it did. Do you think that you'll try again?"

"With her?"

"With anyone."

"I doubt it. My parents' marriage is a long way short of being happy, and my marriage went the same way, mainly because they figured that they knew more about my wife – and my life – than I did. What about you? Do you have a suitable partner now?"

"Unfortunately, no."

"How many relationships have you had so far?"

"None. I've had plenty of affairs, but nothing that lasted long enough to be called a relationship."

"Are you still looking?"

"Of course. The hunt continues."

"Well, I hope that it ends soon."

As the journey continued, Jon's thoughts goed back to the last time that Margaret, his father's mother, visited. He beed 14 at the time, and it beedn't long after his other grandmother haved died. His mother beed far from happy about the visit, but arrive Margaret doed, and maked herself comfortable in his mother's chair in the living room.

After five days, his mother announced that she needed to take the family car to get a few things before the shops closed at 5:30. Just after 6:00, his father arrived home from work, and at 6:30, he walked to the shops. "I cannot find her or the car," he sayed when he returned soon after 7:00. "The police are looking for her."

"Where could she have gone?" Margaret asked.

"I have no idea, Mum. Did she say anything to you?"

"She didn't say anything to me, Joe."

"Jon, did she say anything to you?"

"Nothing, Dad," he replied.

"Think, Jon. There must be something that she said."

"No. There's nothing."

"What did you talk about when you got home from school?"

"Nothing."

"That's true, Joe," Margaret sayed. "She hardly said anything to me the whole day, and all that she said to Jon when he got home from school is for him to go and do his homework."

"When did this start happening?" Joe asked.

"Only today. It must be something that I said, but I cannot imagine what it is."

"Andrea has done some strange things, but I never thought that she would do anything like this. Well, I suppose that I should throw something together."

"Oh, let me do the cooking, Joe. It's the least that I can do."

Early the next morning, Jon beed still in bed when his father entered the room. "Your mother hasn't come home. Look, I've been meaning to have this conversation with you for some time, and this is as good a time as any. Is it true that you don't like me?"

Jon stared at his father for some seconds. "Dad ... what makes you think that I don't?"

"It's written all over your face. You can't even look me in the eye."

Jon locked his eyes just below his father's.

"What has your mother said about me?"

"Nothing, Dad."

"Jon, look me in the eye and tell me again."

"She didn't say anything before she got in the car."

"I'm not talking about yesterday. I'm talking about over the years."

It taked a while before Jon spoke. "You used to hit her when I wasn't around."

"I see. What else?"

"You don't give her enough money to keep the house."

"Interesting. Anything else?"

"You don't take her out often enough."

"Is that what she said?"

"Well, something like that."

"Think carefully, Jon. I want something better than 'something like that'."

"Yeah, it's … She doesn't want to go out with you."

"Because?"

"Because you make her feel embarrassed in front of her friends."

"I see. Thank you, Jon, for leveling with me. Now I'm going to level with you. It's your mother who told me that you don't like me – many times. I don't know whether you do or you don't, but I think that you're old enough to know a few things. First, I've never hit your mother – and I never will. Second, your mother gets more than enough money to keep this house and to take care of her own needs. I've always made sure that all of us get the other things that we need. Don't I?"

"Yes, you do, Dad."

"Finally, we both have to accept that your mother thinks that she and her family are a class above my family. She is always critical of us and our friends, especially your Korean friend. You don't seem to have many friends, but I advise you not to bring any of them home. Okay?"

"I don't, Dad. I learned that from James before he left home. She blames you for that."

"Does she? The truth is that she drove James out of the house. You don't know how many times that I got home from work, and the first thing that I heard is 'Do you know what James did today?' I regret what I did to James as a result, and he understands that."

"Where is he now?"

"I wish that I knew, Jon. I suppose that you know that he went and stayed with my parents in Melbourne, and that he soon upped and left. No one knows where."

"Didn't the police look for him?"

"He was 16 at the time."

"Mother is a lot more than 16 now."

"This is a little different, don't you think?"

"I suppose so."

"Anyway, I'm glad that we've had this conversation. Please, don't tell your mother about it."

When Joe leaved his son's room and goed into the kitchen, Margaret beed sitting at the table. "Joe, I have no idea of what I did wrong," she sayed.

"You've done nothing wrong, Mum," he replied.

"I shouldn't have come. I only came because her mother died. I thought that it's the right thing to do."

"I thought so too."

"I think that I better go."

"You don't need to."

"No, I should go. Just let me pack and I'll catch a bus to the station."

"Nothing doing, Mum. We're going in by taxi."

There beed not many persons on the platform as Margaret beed about to board the train. "Feel free to visit us at any time you like, Mum," Joe sayed.

Just then, Andrea appeared. "I knew that I would find you here. And I'm pleased that you're going back to Melbourne. You don't know how much of a strain it has been on me since my mother died."

"Where the hell were you last night?"

"I stayed in a hotel in Bathurst. Here's the bill if you don't believe me."

"Oh, I believe you all right. What I cannot believe is that you could walk out on us like that."

"I should have done it years ago, Joe. The only reason that I stayed is because of Jon."

"Jon, get your grandmother onto the train, and stay with her until you have to get off. You will find your mother and me out in the car park – somewhere."

On the way to Hidey High, Joe drove the car while Andrea drove the argument, finishing it with "I'm going to leave you, Joe. Soon. And I'm taking Jon with me. He's mine." The rest of the journey beed in silence.

When they stopped in the school car park, Joe turned to Jon, "Let's go." Then to his wife, "I'm leaving the keys in the car, Andrea. If you get any silly ideas about driving off, you can keep driving, and don't bother about coming back."

The vice principal then beed Tim Atherton, who also looked over the top of his glasses when talking. "I hope that whatever the problem is, this is not going to become a habit, Mr. Mamjjasond."

"It's certainly not my intention, Mr. Atherton."

"All right, I'll write your boy a note. Who's your teacher now, Jon?"

'It had to be Maurice Bloody Hoare,' Jon thought to himself as he moved out to get past a slow-moving truck. He looked over at Brent who beed asleep. 'Great company.'

When he entered the classroom, he beed meeted with "Oh, good afternoon, Mamjacent. I'm so pleased that you could join us."

"My name is still Mamjjasond, sir," Jon sayed as handed over the note and taked his place.

Jon beed disappointed to see the car when he arrived home after school, and he goed through the back door and into his room, closed the door, and getted his books out. No more soon haved he started on maths, Andrea opened the door and walked in.

"I've got homework," he sayed.

"Well, it can wait," beed the reply. "We need to talk."

"I have nothing to say to you."

"What were your father and grandmother saying about me last night?"

"Excuse me, I missed a couple of classes this morning, and I also have a lot of homework to do."

"You're not answering my question."

"You're right. I'm not. Now will you please leave and let me get on with my homework?"

"How dare you speak to your mother like that?"

Jon throwed his pen down and turned around. "You're my mother? The one who drives off and abandons us?"

"Just a minute ..."

"If you decide to drive off again, I will not be with you."

"Look, Jon, you don't understand what I'm going through, and I don't expect you to. All that I'm asking for is a bit more support."

"Support for what?"

"Jon, ever since your father pushed James out of the house ..."

"Who did?"

"So, that's what you three have been talking about. Right, your father has a lot of explaining to do."

"I don't think so. It's you who drove him out of the house. Now, I would like to get on with my homework. Possible?"

"Jon ..."

"Obviously not." He threw his books into his bag and standed up. "Now you're driving me out of the house."

"Where do you think you're going?"

"I'm going to the public library!"

"What are you thinking about?" Brent asked.

"Oh, welcome back," Jon replied. "Are you hungry?"

"Where are we?"

"We're getting close to Gundagai. Do you want to see the dog?"

"I've seen it plenty of times, but let's stop there. My shout. I mean: my treat."

"Yes, I know what 'shout' means. Thanks."

"My pleasure. Listen, I'm sorry that I went to sleep back there. It's a long flight from San Francisco."

"You live in Melbourne, right?"

"Ah, you finally guessed. Yes, I live in Melbourne."

"Then why didn't you fly back to Melbourne?"

"I got a special deal, but only from Sydney. I took the train to Sydney, but I don't have enough to get the train back again. Thanks for picking me up. Listen, if you want a place to stay in Melbourne, you would be very welcome to stay with me."

"Well, thanks, but ..."

"If."

"Sure."

"Do you want to talk about it?"

"What?"

"You were deep in thought for quite a while."

"I suppose that I was. There's really nothing to talk about."

"Family, right?"

"Yes, family. I don't want to bore you with the details."

"Can I bore you with how things went with my family? If you don't mind."

"Sure. We still have a long way to go."

Just like YeongTae, but for different reasons, Brent also had a troubled childhood. "By the way," he finished, "my name is Barry Entwhistle. But I prefer that you call me Brent."

"I'm Jon Mamjjasond – with two J's. And I prefer that you call me Jon."

When they reached Melbourne, Jon insisted on taking Brent to his house, and Brent insisted that Jon come in for a few minutes.

"I can't, Brent," Jon sayed. "I need to get over to my parents."

"At this time? Don't you think that it's a bit late? Why don't you call them now?"

"**W**hy are you calling at this time?" Andrea asked. "You could have woken your father, and you know that he's not well. You should have called before now, and you should be here now. Where are you?"

"In Melbourne, Mother."

"Yes, but where in Melbourne?"

"Collingwood."

"What are you doing in Collingwood? Whatever it is, keep doing it. It's far too late to come here now."

"Okay, Mother dear. I'll see you in the morning."

"We'll be at church in the morning. You better come for lunch."

As Jon hanged up the phone, he looked at Brent. "Can I take you up on your offer?"

"Of course. I suppose that you want the spare bed."

"What do you want for breakfast?" Brent asked in the morning. "I've got nothing in the house, so I'll have to go down to the corner shop." When he returned, "I could only get bread."

"That's fine," Jon replied.

"Tell me something. You went to school in Sydney, and your parents live in Melbourne. When did they move?"

"Last year. My father was transferred."

"Oh, I see."

'No, you don't see,' Jon thought to himself.

Joe developed an illness that he more late found out be called Borreliosis, possibly caused by being bited by a bug when he beed cleaning out the garage. Three weeks after, he developed what seemed to be a heavy cold, and when he goed to his family doctor, he beed telled that he beed fit and healthy, and beed gived a note that sayed that he needed a week off work.

The same happened the following week and the week after before he collapsed with severe pain at church and beed taked to a hospital. The doctor who eventually attended to him taked blood tests and telled him that he just passed out, to go home and rest, and that the pain would pass.

It doedn't. The following morning, Joe beed in so much pain that he couldn't get out of bed, and he asked Andrea to call his boss and ask for another day off. On the Wednesday, the boss sayed that he needed another note from the doctor, and that he haved to be back at work at the start of the following week.

On the Friday, he still couldn't get out of bed. This not only costed him his job, but also what little beed leaved of his wife's sympathy and understanding.

During the next school holidays, Jon drived Joe to Melbourne to stay with Margaret and her husband Julius. When he returned to Kurropnagroopna, he finded that his mother haved moved in.

With teaching and a marriage not being as satisfying as he would have liked, and a mother that beed making things more bad, Jon haved to choose between depression and freedom. He eventually choosed the latter. He quitted teaching, leaved his wife and Kurropnagroopna, and leaved his mother with no choice but to move down to Melbourne.

"Come back, Jon," Brent sayed.

"What?"

"Listen, mate, you're thinking too much. Past has passed, and whatever happened cannot be changed. Let it go."

5

The rain beed heavy as Jon parked in the street, and he maked a run to the front door and knocked. "You could have rung the bell," Andrea sayed as she opened the door.

"Sorry, Mother. I didn't see it."

"There's the button right there. Anyway, what was so important that you couldn't get here on time?"

"You wouldn't understand, Mother."

"No, that's true. Anything that you do now is beyond anyone's understanding. I suppose that you want to see your father."

"Isn't that what I'm here for?"

"Well, you better go easy on him. He is not a well man."

"You've already made that quite clear, Mother dear. Where are …?"

"Your grandmother and grandfather are still at the church. They'll be back soon. Your father is in the study. Just go easy on him."

When Jon entered the study, he beed surprised to see Joe wearing a heavy jacket. "I know that it's cold today, but it's not that cold."

"It is for me, Jon. Ever since I got this illness, I feel the cold terribly."

"You still have the illness? You're looking good."

"That's the problem. I look healthy, but I'm not. All that I get from the doctors is that I need to drink lots of water and the problem will soon pass."

"But you are better."

"Not that much better. I still have pain all over my body, I hardly ever have a good night's sleep, I feel tired all the time, and I'm extremely sensitive to light and sound. It doesn't matter which doctor I go to, I'm told that I must be making things up. To make things worse, your mother keeps saying the same thing. What are you looking at me like that for? You should know me well enough to know that I don't make things up. Don't you?"

"I don't remember it ever happening. Dad, how long have these doctors been practicing?"

"Over twenty years."

"It sounds like they need more practice. Anyway, why am I here?"

Joe hesitated. "Look, you don't have a job now, do you? Or a wife and children."

Jon looked straight at his father. "Are you asking me to move in here?"

"Jon, I cannot do a lot of the things that I could do before. This is not a new house as you can see, and it does need a lot of maintenance. Your grandfather is too old for it, and now I'm too ill to do it."

"Dad, isn't it obvious to you that I don't want to live with Mother ever again?"

"Look, I understand how you feel, but can't you put what has happened between you and her in the past?"

"Have you asked James?"

"Jon, you know as well as anyone that he had bigger issues with your mother, and I can't very well ask him to move here from Perth. Look, I don't want to impose on you."

"Can't you move to Perth?"

"It's not that simple. It would be a lot easier for you to move down here."

"Dad, I need to move to a place where I can get a job."

"Jon, whatever you're looking for, you have as much chance of finding it in any Australian city. All that I'm suggesting is that you look around in Melbourne where at least you have somewhere to stay."

"Dad, I'm thinking about teaching in Korea."

"I hope that you mean South Korea."

"Yes. South Korea."

"I see. Tell me something. What makes you think that you won't have the same problems there as you had in Australia? And if you do, will you then run off to another country?"

"I said that I'm thinking about it, Dad. I haven't made up my mind yet."

"Well, it's your life, and whatever you decide, I don't want to stand in your way. By the way, if you don't mind me asking, where did you stay last night?"

"With a friend."

"I didn't know that you have any friends in Melbourne. Do you think that you can go back there tonight?"

"Aren't I supposed to be staying here?"

"Yes, but …"

"Mother?"

"Well, yes. Look, if you decide to move down to Melbourne, you will be able to stay here, but this time, it's just going to be a little …"

"Don't worry. I'll head back to Sydney this afternoon."

"Look, I don't want you to feel …"

"It's okay, Dad. Don't worry about it."

"Well, okay, if that's what you want to do. You are staying for lunch, aren't you?"

"If it's no problem."

"Come on, don't be like that. I'm sure that your mother has something prepared for the five of us."

"So what have you decided, Jon?" Andrea asked as she served steak and vegetables.

"I haven't yet," he replied.

"Well, I hope that you realize that you cannot stay here."

"Oh, hell's bells, Andrea," Joe sayed. "We've talked about this, and we agreed that he could sleep in the third bedroom. What's the problem now?"

"The problem, Joe, is that you would be in the second bedroom with me, and I wouldn't get any rest."

Joe looked at Jon. "I'm sorry that you wasted your weekend, Jon. Perhaps you should go to Korea."

"Korea? What's in Korea?"

"He could be teaching there."

"Oh, fine. So you're going to run off and abandon us – again."

"I have never abandoned you!" Jon sayed.

"Don't shout at the table, Jon."

"I'm not shouting at the table, and I'm not shouting at you. You know that I have never abandoned you."

"Well, you're about to abandon us now."

"As I said before, Mother dear, I haven't decided yet."

As he leaved Melbourne behind him, his mind goed back to the month that he quitted the teaching post at Kurropnagroopna, separated from his wife, and goed back to Sydney and rented a small room in the back garden of a house not far from Hidey High. He could do anything that he liked there provided it beed legal, and that included throwing things around the room, punching the walls, and crying himself to sleep at night.

When he doed get to sleep, he often dreamed about going to Melbourne, and instead of seeing his parents, he beed walking the streets not far out of the central business district.

It suddenly occurred to him that he could have dreamed about streets in Collingwood. Should he turn back and see Brent? 'Not now. I need to know more about Korea.'

He knowed that when he beed suffering from depression, he figured that a doctor would most likely recommend drugs. Even though some of his friends at college haved beed on drugs, Jon feeled proud that he haved never taked any, and that he never would.

6

On Monday morning, Jon knocked at Neil Drummond's door. "I've come to see Mr. Kang."

"Let me check the schedule. Oh, I'm afraid that he has classes all morning, but you can see him at break time. Would you like to sit down?"

"It's okay. I can come back this afternoon."

"Actually, I'm glad that you called in. Have you decided anything about Korea?"

"Not yet. That's why I want to see Mr. Kang."

"Fair enough. Jon, it seems that you enjoyed being at this school."

"Not really, sir."

"Oh? You got good results all the way through, except for English in grade eight."

"I think that you know why, sir."

"Mr. Hoare?"

"Exactly. All the other teachers were good – they always tried to understand their students. Hoare never did."

"What about you? When you were teaching, I mean."

"I did my best to understand my students, only to find that most of them had no interest in trying to understand me."

"Things have changed in the last ten years, Jon."

"Yes, sir. I know."

"Look, I would like to suggest something to you. We have a teacher here who comes from Zimbabwe. Apparently they are screaming for qualified teachers in most subject areas including English. Perhaps you should talk with her. She's free now, so let me introduce you to her."

"I don't know how Neil getted the impression that Zimbabwe need English teachers," Ingrid sayed after Neil haved leaved her office. "What they do need be teachers of mathematics and science."

"That's not me," Jon replied.

"Even if it beed you, I would think very carefully before going there. In the mission school that I beed sended to, even though I haved no religious beliefs, there beed a maths teacher from Australia who beed throwed out of the country, all because he agreed to support a student in his last two years at the school."

"What happened?"

"Long story short: Simbai's family doedn't have enough money to send him to high school, and so a teacher at the local primary school offered to do so in return for working in his fields after school and on weekends. But then that teacher died, and his wife haved no intention of supporting Simbai the following year, and she doedn't want anyone else to support him. Nor doed the principal, and when it becomed clear that Roger beedn't going to back down, two of his female students goed to his room late at night asking for help with their maths. But instead of opening their books, they opened their shirts, and screamed that Roger tried to have sex with them. The principal sended for the police, and Roger beed gived twenty-four hours to leave the country."

"What happened to …?"

"Simbai beed registered at a school about fifty kilometers away."

"How could that have happened?"

Ingrid smiled.

"You registered him."

"Correct. But then the principal found out about it, and when the students goed on strike about several other matters, I beed accused of starting it. Of course, he haved no proof, but I decided that I either get transferred to a government school or I would quit. With no support from my family, my husbands' families, or the education officials, I quitted, leaved Simbai with more than enough to complete his high school education, and comed to Australia with my son."

"How often do you hear from Simbai?"

"We be still in touch. When he finished high school, he getted a job with a trading company in Harare. He wanted to pay me back, but it be difficult to send money out of Zimbabwe. Not only that, he have his future to think of."

"What about Roger?"

"Nothing. I think that he wanted to forget about the whole thing and move on."

"I wouldn't blame him. Ingrid, the English that you use: is that the standard in Zimbabwe?"

"Oh, no. It be British English in most of southern Africa. I only started to talk like this when I comed to Australia and finded myself teaching special English to kids from other countries who need it."

"Like YeongTae Kim."

"You know him?"

"Since last Thursday."

"Oh, so you be the one who picked him up on the Hume Highway."

"That's me."

Just then, the bell ringed.

"It be break time," she said. "Do you mind if we see Mark together?"

"The schools and universities in Korea don't start for a couple of weeks," Mark sayed, "and the better ones have already appointed their teachers for this year. There are also private schools which are supposed to provide extra instruction for exams and conversation practice, but quite a few of them don't pay their teachers on time if at all, and I don't know anyone who's in any of the better ones."

"So there be nothing good in Korea at the moment," Ingrid sayed.

"I'm not saying that. I've got an American friend who's the director of the English language program at a university in Seoul, and I'm sure that you would be treated fairly, Jon. I can call him tonight if you like."

Just then, there beed a knock at the door. "Come in. YeongTae! Something wrong?"

"Hoare: he tried to make me do the test again. I doedn't prepare for it because I thinked that I doedn't have to do it."

"You doedn't," Ingrid sayed. "That beed maked very clear to everyone at the meeting last week. What the hell be wrong with that man?"

"Did you do it?" Mark asked.

"No, sir," YeongTae replied.

"What did you do?"

"I wanted to read the book, but he taked it off me, so I taked out my maths and he tried to take that off me."

"Tried."

"I standed up, and he pushed me back into my seat and tried again to take my maths books. Sir, my maths exercise book be now teared."

"Let me see it. Oh, that's not good. Let's go and see Mr. Drummond now. Do you want to join us, Ingrid?"

"Absolutely," Ingrid replied.

"Well, YeongTae, before I make a decision, I need to hear the other side of the story," Neil sayed after a while. "Go to your next class, and come back here at the start of lunch. Oh, before you do, could you ask Jon to come and see me now?"

"I've done nothing wrong, Neil," Maurice sayed as he entered Neil's office.

"Sit down, Maurice."

"I have a class now."

"Please sit down."

As Maurice doed so, Jon arrived.

"Please, sit down, Jon."

"I prefer to stand, sir," Jon replied, looking at Maurice.

"Okay, sure. Jon, as you are a trained teacher of English, would you be willing to take the 8A English class that's about to start?"

"Neil, you've got to be joking," Maurice sayed.

"Would you, Jon?"

Jon and Maurice stared at each other.

"It would be a pleasure, sir," Jon sayed.

"This is crazy!" Maurice sayed. "He doesn't have any idea of what they're doing."

"I will find out soon enough. With all due respect, Mr. Hoare, I doubt that you've had any idea of what you've been doing ever since you started teaching."

"Now, look here," Maurice sayed as he standed up, but when Jon taked a step toward him, he sitted down again.

"Thanks, Jon," Neil sayed. "There's the bell. Good luck."

Jon smiled as he leaved the office.

"This is absolutely crazy," Maurice sayed. "How the hell could you put the likes of him in charge of a class?"

Neil leaned back in his chair, taked off his glasses, and stared at Maurice. "The likes of him. What exactly are the likes of him?"

"You know what I mean."

"No, Maurice, I don't know what you mean."

"Neil, his grades for English in my class were not good."

"Were not good. Does that mean that they're good now?"

"All right, I mean that they are not good."

"Here's the thing: the only class in which Jon's grades are not good is yours, and it's the same for many other students over the years. Maurice, didn't you agree that YeongTae doesn't need to do that test again?"

"No, Neil. I didn't agree."

"All right, didn't I make it clear that YeongTae doesn't need to do that test again?"

"But you're not an English teacher."

Neil stared at Maurice for some seconds. "No, Maurice, I'm only the vice principal of this school. I'm the one who has received many complaints about you, and yet I have defended you every time. Every bloody time, Maurice. And yet you have the nerve to sit there and tell me that because I'm not an English teacher, you don't have to follow my instructions if you don't agree with them."

"I didn't say that."

"YeongTae Kim went into Ingrid's classes hating English because of the teachers that he had in Korea. Within two months – two months, Maurice – he was loving English. Was, because he's back to hating English. Now why is that?"

"Look, Neil, my job is to bring students up to standard. Am I wrong?"

"You're not wrong, but what really interests me now is why you told YeongTae to do the test again even though he reached the standard. Please explain."

"Because he has never reached the standard before."

"And so you think that he copied."

"Yes."

"Who was sitting next to him in the test?"

"Brian Harris."

"What mark did he get?"

"I'll have to check that."

"That's what you said on Friday. Now, I understand that you tore YeongTae's maths exercise book. Why?"

"I didn't tear it. Look, Neil, it was an accident. These things happen."

"Here's what's going to happen, Maurice: I'm taking YeongTae out your class. He will need the time to write up a new maths exercise book anyway. Here's what isn't going to happen: when a parent comes to me to complain about you, I will not defend you. I will send them straight to your classroom or your office."

"Good. Bring it on."

"Fine. Well, I'm about to go round and see how Jon's getting on. You're welcome to join me."

When Jon seed Neil and Maurice at the door, he walked across and opened it. "This is a really good class. Would you like to come in and hear them making up a story as they go along?"

"I'd love to," Neil sayed. "Maurice?"

"Pass," Maurice sayed as he walked off.

At the start of lunch, Neil beed in his usual place at the head of the table with YeongTae and Mark to his left, and Jon and Peter to his right. "Jon has agreed to take over from Maurice once Maurice either transfers or quits. I don't know which it is because he has just decided to go on sick leave."

"For how long?" Mark asked. "And for what reason?"

"Only for today, I hope, and the reason is stress."

"He brought that on himself."

"That's how it appears, but there's more to it, which I'm not prepared to discuss here. I think that you know that sick leave has to be paid out of the school's budget, and long service leave doesn't, so I intend to have him start his long service leave tomorrow."

"And when he comes back?"

"Well, I'm hoping that his replacement will still be here then."

"Is that you?" Mark asked, looking at Jon.

Jon smiled.

"So you will be my English teacher?" YeongTae asked.

"Absolutely," Jon sayed. "And you can talk however you like, just so long as you're understood."

"Jon, that's not …" Neil started.

"Neil … Can I call you that?"

"Yes, of course, but …"

"Neil, Hoare has obviously never kept himself up to date on how English is meant to be taught. The focus now is on communication skills, not on being 'correct' in everything that you say. Those kids in 8A have great imaginations, and I just wish that I had recorded their story today."

"So you won't be going to Korea at any time soon," Mark sayed.

"No, Mark," Jon replied. "I'm sorry if I troubled you."

"You haven't troubled me at all. It simply means that I don't need to call my contact tonight."

"Perhaps Maurice Hoare could take a position there," Neil said.

"Perhaps he could, but it won't be through me."

"Fair enough. Well, I think that's it, gentlemen. Any questions?"

"Mr. Drummond, why be I at this meeting?" YeongTae asked.

"Good question. I was going to take you out of Mr. Hoare's class, but now there's no need. Unless you make trouble for Mr. Mamjjasond."

"I doedn't make trouble with Mr. Hoare, sir."

"No, indeed you didn't, YeongTae. Indeed you didn't."

7

As Jon headed out of Sydney for the two-week Easter break, he feeled happy. He beed enjoying his classes and the atmosphere of his old school, and he haved an agreement to visit his parents and grandmother during the school vacations. He doed, however, regret that he beed on a contract for the rest of the year instead of being a permanent teacher again, but perhaps it beed just as well.

There beed only two students in the school who doedn't like him: YeongTae's brothers in 9A and 10B. They continued to give him the same look as they gived when they first meeted near their home. They beedn't in any of his classes, and the only problem that he haved with them be when he finded them smoking near the football field. The exchange beed about to turn physical when he backed off and reported the matter to Neil. The meeting the next day revealed two more who doedn't like him: the parents who maked it clear that any contact with YeongTae outside of the school could result in some degree of violence. Jon beed proud of his physical abilities, but he haved a pretty good idea of the limits.

Despite his intention not to pick anyone up, Jon stopped for an Aboriginal guy who beed walking on the side of the limited access road. "Where to?" he asked.

"Kurropnagroopna," comed the reply.

"Jump in. I'm heading to Melbourne, so I can drop you at the turn off for Wagga. Better still, how about I drop you off in Wagga?"

"Thanks." As they started moving, "So you know where Kurropnagroopna is."

"I should do. I was there for six years."

"At the high school?"

"That's right."

"Are you Mr. Mamjacket?"

"Mamjjasond. Jon Mamjjasond. You are?"

"Phillip Gray, but everyone calls me Skybee."

"As in: the sky be gray."

"Right."

"Why not Skyiz, as in: the sky is gray?"

"It doesn't sound as good, does it? Besides, I know that there are some Americans who would say that the sky be gray."

"I know a teacher and a student in Sydney who would also say it like that."

"Do you remember Jody Greggs?"

"Sure. He was in my grade ten class last year."

"He's my cousin. He used to say that you're one of the best teachers that he ever had."

"Well, he's one of a few who did, but something happened that changed his attitude. I asked him a few times about it, but I never got a friendly answer."

"What do you think happened?"

"I have no idea. All I know is that he left home one morning and never got to school. After that, his attitude was very different."

"Yeah, well, his parents think that it's something sexual. What else could it be?"

"Who knows? It could be sexual; it could be anything. Whatever it is, he needs to talk with somebody. He can't keep it inside himself for the rest of his life. How's he going with grade 11?"

"He's not. As far as I know, he's still looking for a job. His father told him to get back to school but he says that it's a waste of time."

"What do you think?"

"Me?"

"Yeah. Did you do grade 11?"

"No. I had to go out and work. My father walked out on us when I was in grade ten, and I was the oldest in the family – aside from my parents, of course."

"I guess that you still are."

"Yeah. You're right. I got a job in a furniture factory. Metal walls, metal roof: bloody hot in summer; bloody cold in winter. A boss that pushed us hard. But the pay was okay."

"There's a furniture factory in Kurropnagroopna?"

"There was. It's gone now."

"How long did you stay in that job?"

"Four years – up until the factory closed down. Then I got a job training horses."

"In Kurropnagroopna?"

"No, near to where you picked me up."

"So you train horses for racing?"

"No, we train horses for riding. There's nothing taught at school that's useful for that. Tell me something. Do you teach Shakespeare with all of its out-of-date language?"

"No, I ..."

"That's good, but I suppose you teach literature about nice people doing nice things in nice environments."

"Were you taught anything like that at school?"

"I don't know. I didn't pay much attention."

"There are no novels about people and things being nice all the time, simply because no one would read them. Tell me of one movie or television drama that you've seen or heard about that doesn't have a conflict situation in it."

"Yeah, okay. Fair enough."

"Look, I help students to be able to express their opinions clearly, and we look at novels that are about reality – what really goes on in the world."

"How about what went on in Australia 200 years ago? The way that the British came and took over this land, brought their diseases, dumped their criminals here, pushed most of my people onto reserves, and let them live in housing that's way below standard? How about our people being denied the right to vote until twenty-something years ago? Have you looked at any novels about how your people introduced alcohol to my people and called them drunks? How about the way that you white people take all of the good jobs? How about the way that the government and the church took kids away from our families and put them with your families?"

"To be honest …"

"You haven't, have you?"

"No. I tried to get an Aboriginal author into the course last year, but the head of the English department wouldn't approve it. I should have got somebody else to ask her."

"Are you talking about Willis?"

"That's the one. Betty Willis."

"Well, there's an excellent example of why I found school to be a waste of time. She hated me, and I hated her. When I had English with her, I spent more time in the vice principal's office."

"So you're not the best person to convince Jody to go back to school."

"Guess not."

"Who is?"

After a pause, "No one."

Just after Jon turned onto the highway to Wagga, he looked at Skybee. "Gray is not your real name, is it? I mean that some time down the generations, your family name became Gray."

"My family lost their real names about four generations ago."

"Do you know what those names are?"

"No idea. No one knows or they're not telling. Do you know where your name comes from?"

"I think that it has something to with a climate chart."

"A what?"

"I'm J F Mamjjasond. That's J F M-A-M-J-J-A-S-O-N-D. If you look at a climate chart, that's what you see for the months of the year. I'm Jonathan Frederick Mamjjasond, my brother is James Frederick Mamjjasond, my father is Joseph Francis Mamjjasond, his father is Julius Francis Mamjjasond, and back it goes."

"That's interesting. Can I ask you a favor? Could you drop me on the other side of Wagga? I can get a ride more easily there."

"How about I drop you off in Narrandera? It should be even easier to get a ride to Kurropnagroopna from there."

"All right, but only if you let me shout you lunch there."

"Where were you intending to have lunch?" Jon asked as they were about to go through Narrandera.

"At home," Skybee replied.

"Do you think that there can be a place for one more?"

"You want to come to Kurropnagroopna?"

"Sure. I would like to catch up with Jody – if it's possible."

"You won't change his mind."

"Skybee, I've come this far."

"I know you," Mary Gray sayed as he extended her hand. "You're the one who taught English to Jody's class last year."

Jon taked the hand. "Tried to. He was doing well for a while until he went missing for a day. After that … Anyway, I want to talk with him."

"You should have talked with him last year."

"I tried, Mrs. Gray."

"Oh, you can call me Mary. Anyway, let's have lunch."

Just like Skybee, Mary also haved broad shoulders and thick arms. Jon wondered if they comed about with working or if it be natural. Probably both, he concluded.

After being introduced to Skybee's more young brother and two sisters, they sitted down at the kitchen table. Over soup and sandwiches, they talked about the high school: how most of the teachers gived Skybee a hard time, and how the administration doedn't care.

"I think that Jody should keep looking for work," Mary sayed. "If he goes back to the school now, the teachers will give him worse treatment than they did before."

"Yeah, Mum, but where are the jobs in this place?" Skybee asked.

"He needs to look somewhere else. What about where you're working?"

"I asked, but there's nothing there. I'm lucky to have got that job."

"You enjoy it, don't you?"

"I love it, Mum. I've told you that."

"I'm just worried that one day, something bad is going to happen to you. Jon, where are you going after this?"

"Melbourne," he replied.

"You're welcome to sleep here before you go down there. Perhaps you wouldn't mind a passenger."

"**I** just want to make sure that you understand this," Jon sayed as he beed about to drive through Narrandera. "The guy that you'll be staying with is gay. Okay?"

"Okay," Jody replied. "He's not going to try anything, is he?"

"He promised me on the phone last night that he won't, and I believe him. But if he does, you're to call me immediately. Okay?"

"Sure. Mr. Mamjjasond …"

"Call me Jon."

"Okay. Jon, I'm sorry about giving you a hard time last year."

"I think that you gave all your teachers a hard time last year."

"Yeah, I did."

After a pause, "What happened, Jody?"

"What do you mean?"

"I mean that you were one of the top students in my class, you took a day off, and then you behaved like most of the others."

"I don't want to talk about it. Can we talk about something else?"

"Yes, we can. I'm open to almost anything."

"Let's talk about sex."

"What? No. I said almost anything. Not that."

"Maybe it's because you don't know nothing about sex."

"Is that what you think? Actually, that's quite correct: I don't know nothing about sex. Which I think is the opposite to you: you do know nothing about sex."

"Oh, ha ha. You're still an English teacher."

"I'm a lot of things, Jody, and so are you. You can be anything that you want to be – once you can escape your past. Jody, sorry, but you've got to get it all out in the open.

Learn from your mistakes. This is how I know so much, because I've made more mistakes than most people. I made a hell of a lot of mistakes in my first year of teaching. I could blame the teachers college for not giving enough preparation, but what's the point?"

"But you quit because of us."

"Not only you and most of the other students. I had no support from Willis, my marriage was a disaster, and looking back, I can see that I'm not exactly free from blame. Everyone makes mistakes, and we need to learn from them and move on."

There beed silence for a while.

"Answer me one thing, Jody," Jon continued. "Is what you did on the day of your absence from school illegal? Yes or no."

"Aren't we going to Melbourne?"

"Yes, we are."

"Then why are we going this way?"

"This is the Newell Highway, Jody. Can you think of a faster way to get to Melbourne?"

"No."

"So is what you did on the day of your absence from school illegal? Just give me a yes or no."

"I don't know."

"Jody, if what you did is illegal, then we have to go to the police."

"Then the answer is no."

"Okay, the answer is no, which means that we don't have to go to the police."

"Do we have to keep talking about this?"

"No. No, we don't. Let's talk about football. Do you follow the Australian Football League?"

"Sure. My team is Collingwood."

"Because they won the first AFL Grand Final last year?"

"Because of their colors."

"Black and white aren't colors."

"I know that. I did like science. Well, some of it."

As they headed south to Victoria, science and other school subjects beed discussed. When they getted around to English, "You know, you wrote some great essays, especially about your experiences living in a town where there can be trouble between Black kids and White shop owners," Jon sayed.

"You think that it didn't happen?"

"I had heard about it before I had any idea that I would be posted to Kurropnagroopna High. Even if I hadn't, the way that you wrote your essays told me that it did happen. You got A's because you deserved A's."

"Until that day that I missed school."

"I wasn't going to mention that."

"But you were leading up to it."

"Jody, you don't want to talk about it, and I respect that. It wasn't my intention to lead up to it. Okay?"

There beed no reply, so Jon turned on the car radio and eventually picked up a station in Shepparton. When the news comed on, Jon tried for another station before turning the radio off. Jody haved falled asleep.

"**O**h, you do manage to find the good-looking ones," Brent remarked when he opened his front door. "Don't worry, kid. You're too young."

Jody looked at Jon.

"Brent, you haven't exactly put Jody at ease."

"Oh, I'm sorry. But if I'm saying it, I'm sure that his girlfriends are also saying it."

"I'm sure that they are. Listen, Jody would like to sleep in the living room. Possible?"

"Well, yes, but the spare bed is more comfortable."

"I know. Is it okay if I sleep there?"

"I thought that you're sleeping at your parents' house."

"That was the arrangement last time, but it didn't work out."

"Where did you sleep?"

"Back in Sydney."

"You could have stayed here."

"I know, and I should have. Anyway, I have a feeling that the arrangement could fall through again."

"You have an interesting family, Jon. So when do you think that you will come back here?"

"I'll try for half past six. And I'll bring pizza."

"Okay. Jody, what would you like to do?"

"I want to see the Collingwood Football Ground," Jody replied. "If you tell me how to get there, I'll find it."

"I can drop you off there," Jon sayed.

"No, I've never been in Melbourne before. I want to look around."

8

"Why is it that you can never get here when you say you will?" be the first thing that his mother sayed when he arrived.

"I did call ahead, Mother. Besides, weren't you at church this morning?"

"Your father is too ill to go to church now, and he could have done with the company. I suppose that you were in Collingwood last night."

"No, Mother, I wasn't."

"Then where were you?"

"If I answer, would that end this line of questioning?"

"Oh, don't tell me if it causes you that much shame. Look, there's a lot of work to be done around here, especially since your grandfather died. You better go and see your father – in the study. Go easy on him."

"Of course. And I feel no shame in whatever I do."

"I heard your little exchange out there," Joe sayed, "and your mother is right: I could have done with some company this morning."

"Sorry, Dad. Anyway, how are you feeling?"

"Same as before."

"So nothing has changed."

"There are only two things that have changed for me. One is that I'm not seeing doctors anymore. All that I've got from them, after sitting in the waiting room for anything up to an hour, is that Borreliosis doesn't exist in Australia, and that all the pain and suffering that I feel 24/7 are simply imagination. One doctor got really angry with me when I suggested that I have Borreliosis. I demanded my money back, but of course he refused."

"I hope that I will never have to depend on doctors."

"Don't be too critical of them. I'm sure that there are some good doctors out there – somewhere. Son, keep yourself fit and strong for as long as you can. You won't regret it."

"I know, and that's what I'm doing. What's the other thing that has changed for you?"

"Your mother has finally become a bit more reasonable about my situation. Son, I'm glad that you're teaching again and that it's in Australia. Are you enjoying it?"

"It's great. I didn't realize before that the quality of the administration in a school can make such a difference. "

"I'm glad to hear it. I assume that you mean the principal and vice principal."

"Certainly the vice principal. But back to you. What do you plan to do?"

Joe's voice goed soft. "Go and see where your mother and grandmother are, and come back and close the door gently. I don't want them or anyone else to hear what I'm about to say."

The two ladies beed talking in the kitchen, and they stopped when Jon appeared. "Dad needs a glass of water," he sayed. "Keep talking. Don't let me disturb you."

'How could I possibly disturb them?' he asked himself as he returned to the study. 'Both of them have been disturbed for years.'

"I'm going to get straight to the point, son," Joe sayed in a low voice, "and I need your promise that you will never tell anyone else what I'm about to say. Do I have it?"

"Yes, Dad. You do."

"Thank you. Jon ..." He breathed heavily. "Jon ... it's pretty obvious that I am no longer of any use to anyone, and I ..."

"What do you mean?"

"Exactly what I said. Before you ask, I'm not going to kill myself. I'm too weak for that, and I want to leave this world in peace and with as little trouble to others as possible. What I plan to do is to let nature take its course. There are expensive drugs that I could take which are not covered under the government's medical benefits scheme or under my private health insurance scheme, and there's no guarantee as to how effective they are, how long I'd have to keep taking them, how long they can keep me alive, or if I have enough money. I've made a decision, Jon. The money that I've been able to save up is ultimately for you and James."

"I don't know what to say, Dad."

"There's nothing for you to say. It's my decision, I'm pretty sure that God will accept it, and I want you to accept it. I also want you to accept that your mother will want to have a church funeral, and I want you and James to give the speeches. Okay?"

"Of course."

"Just as a matter of interest, were you with this friend in Collingwood last night?"

"No, Dad, I wasn't." By now, the voice levels beed back to normal.

"You told your mother that you weren't."

"And that's what I'm telling you."

"Then where were you last night?"

"If you must know, I was in Kurropnagroopna."

"What the hell were you doing there? I thought that you didn't want to have anything more to do with the place."

"I suddenly became aware of a loose end that needs attention."

"A loose end. All right. You know what you're doing. At least I hope that you know what you're doing. Just as a matter of interest, how many friends do you have in Sydney? Outside of the school, I mean."

"About twelve less than a dozen."

"And yet you have friends outside of Sydney."

"Where are we going with this, Dad?"

"Just be careful. Okay?"

"I'm always careful. Now, where am I sleeping tonight?"

"I hope that you don't mind in here."

"On the floor."

"Problem?"

"Yeah, I think … Yeah, there is. There's a double bed in the second bedroom. Why can't you and Mother sleep together in that while I'm here, and let me have the bed in the third bedroom?"

"Now that's a bloody good question, and I think that you know the answer."

"Indeed I do. Now, what needs to be done around the house?"

"How's that for timing?" Jon asked when he arrived back at Brent's just after six.

"You said half past six," Brent sayed.

"Right. Half a minute past six. And now it's one minute past six."

"Do you teach your students this?"

"As a matter of fact … no."

"Well, that's a relief. Let's dig into the pizza before it gets cold."

Jon haved just started painting a wall of the garage when his mother comed out. "What are you doing?" she asked. "Are you going to paint the walls like that?"

"No, Mother. I'm going to eat them."

"Don't try to be funny with me. If you're going to do a job, you could at least do it properly."

"I am doing it properly. Look. Here's the paint brush. I put the paint brush into the can of paint, bring it out, and then apply paint to the surface to be painted using long strokes. See? Any questions?"

"Thank you, Jon. What I'm talking about is the color. That's not what I chose."

"I know. This is the first coat and I'm using up old paint."

"Is that what your father told you to do?"

"Yes, it is. Now, can I get on with it? I would like to finish the first coat today."

The next morning beed cold with heavy cloud and a promise of rain. When Jon bringed a ladder inside the house, "What are you doing with that?" Andrea asked.

"I'm carrying it," Jon replied.

"Can't I get a straight answer to anything that I ask?"

"That is a straight answer. I think what you mean to ask is what I intend to do with this, and the answer is that I intend to climb up under the roof to see what needs to be done there."

"Jon!" comed from the study. "Come here!"

Jon putted down the ladder, leaned it against a wall, and goed to the study. "Yes, Dad?"

"Did I say to go into the roof?"

"No, Dad."

"Then why are you doing it?"

"Because it could rain today. All my jobs are outside."

"Have you never worked in the rain before?"

"Well, I've never painted in the rain before. I'm not sure if it's a good idea to mix paint with water."

"It isn't. Nor is climbing into the roof. Do you have any idea of what could have got in there in the last fifty years? When I cleaned out the garage in Sydney, there were newspapers and magazines dating back to 1926, and mouse droppings and dust all over them. Jon, hasn't it occurred to you that what happened to me could happen to you if you go up there? Do you have any idea of what could have got in there in the last fifty years?"

"Well, actually, no. So what do you want me to do?"

"You could check the pipes in both the back and front yards. Water mixes with water quite well."

"So does dirt."

"Oh, so you're afraid of mud now."

"Right, I'll check the pipes."

"You're not coming into the house like that," Andrea sayed at the end of the day.

"How would you like me to come into the house? Perhaps I should climb through the bathroom window."

"That would be better than dropping mud all over the place."

"Mother, I'm cold and wet, and I need to get these clothes off and under a hot shower. Should I take my clothes off out here? Perhaps you could sell tickets to the neighbors. I can do a song and dance if you like."

"Don't be so bloody stupid, Jon. Just get your clothes off and get into the bathroom as quickly as possible."

"Your choice, Mother. You do realize that you could have made a fortune."

The next morning, there beed hardly a cloud in the sky, and Jon wasted no time with getting started on the painting. He haved doed nearly half a wall when Andrea comed out. "What do you think of the color, Jon?" she asked.

"It's fine. You have obviously made an excellent choice." 'Oh, yes. Bright blue is a really wonderful choice,' he thinked to himself.

"No, seriously, Jon. What do you really think?"

"It's great. It will certainly be the talk of the neighborhood."

"If it were your choice, what color would you have picked?"

"I have no idea. I don't live here." 'And I never will.'

"Mum! Have you got a minute?"

Margaret comed out.

"What do you think?"

"I think that Jon's doing a wonderful job."

"The color, I mean."

"I have no opinion, Andrea." She goed back into the house.

"Jon …"

"I'm not changing it, Mother. This is what you insisted on, and this is what you get."

"I want it changed, Jon. If you won't do it, I'll get somebody in who will."

"So once again, my trip down here has been a waste of time."

"What, are you going to run off? To Collingwood, perhaps?"

"Yes, to Collingwood, and then back to Sydney. I hope that you don't mind if I wash out the brushes and put everything away first."

"So you're going to abandon us again, are you?"

"Who abandoned us when I was in grade eight? Answer me that."

"All right, Jon. Just go. And if you think that you can come back here and be waited on hand and foot, you've got another thing coming."

"And what thing is that?"

"What are you talking about?"

"You just said that I've got another thing coming. Can you be more specific?"

"Jon, you're just being stupid again."

"Of course I am. I should have realized that you mean that I have another think coming."

"Look, I told you what I want, and you won't bloody well do it."

"I was doing what you wanted!"

"Don't shout at me. Whatever will the neighbors think?"

"I don't care what they think, or what you bloody think!"

"Jon!" Joe beed standing at the back door. "I want to see you in the study."

"Yes, sir! May I clean up first?"

"This takes priority, Jon."

"Jon, I want you to finish the job. That means sanding down what you've done this morning and applying the new color."

"Two things: I cannot sand down wet paint; and …"

"I'm well aware of that. Look, we both know that your mother is not an easy person to live with."

"You can say that again."

"Jon, you're here for another ten days even if you're not sleeping here. I'm here for the rest of my life which, as you know, may not be that much longer. I'm not going to die a happy man, Jon, and the least that you can do for me is to see the job through."

"What if she changes her mind again. We both know that it has happened before."

"She won't."

"How do you know?"

"I know because your grandmother is going to have the final choice this time. This is her house, after all."

"**Done**," Jon sayed after seven days. "The garage, and the pipes in both yards. Is there anything else before I go?"

"You're leaving today?" Andrea asked.

"If there's nothing else to be done."

"Don't you think that you should spend more time with your father? You must have things to talk about."

"We've talked."

Joe struggled into the kitchen. "There is something else, Jon. Have you got a few minutes?"

"Of course."

In the study: "Jon, it's very likely that I will die before your mother does, and so, in my will, everything that I own will go to her. Otherwise, everything will be shared equally between you and James. Now, I've made sure that your mother's will is the same."

"That when she dies, everything that you own will go to her?"

"Jon, I'm being serious. You know exactly what I mean."

"Sorry, Dad."

"Now, because you quit teaching before, you cannot get a permanent position now. Is that right?"

"It seems that way. Why?"

"Because I have named James as the one to handle the wills when each of us die. As you know, his business is doing very well …"

"I don't know that. How do you know?"

"I know. All right?"

"Wouldn't it be expected that both of us handle the will?"

"So you don't trust him."

"Should I? Who is the one who left home at 16 and left a whole lot of debts for you to pay off?"

"Jon, that's a long time ago. The point is that he is married, and his position is secure. You are no longer married, not even a girlfriend, and your position is not secure. Look, that's my final decision and I don't want to discuss this any further. I hope that I've made myself quite clear."

"Indeed you have, Dad. I'll see you in the next school holidays. And I expect to only have to do a job once and to have a bed to sleep in. I hope that I have made myself quite clear."

"**S**omething wrong, Jon?" Brent asked when he getted home from work.

"I really don't want to talk about it," Jon replied.

"And that's what I keep saying to you," Jody sayed.

"Yeah, but you've been sitting on your situation since last year. I've been … No, you're right, Jody. You're absolutely right. But perhaps we should have dinner first and you can tell us about your job hunt while we're eating."

Jody's job hunt beedn't going well, and he asked Jon if he could take him back to Kurropnagroopna.

"I'm not going back that way," Jon replied.

"But you came that way," Jody sayed.

Jon looked at Brent. "Is there something between you two that I should know about?"

"Nothing that I'm aware of," Brent said. "Jody, you're welcome to stay here for as long as you want."

"Thanks, but I should be paying board," Jody sayed.

"You can when you get a job – if you still want to stay here."

After dinner, Jon telled about his family – from his mother's stay in a hotel in Bathurst to his father's final decision about the wills.

9

Jon felt that there beed something wrong before he walked into the school for the teachers' day at the start of the second term. When he entered the staff room, he sitted next to Mark who beed sitting next to Ingrid.

Ingrid leaned across Mark. "Have you heared about Neil?"

"What about Neil?" Jon replied.

"He was killed in a car accident," Mark sayed.

"What happened?"

"A car was coming the other way on the wrong side of the road. It was on a bend, so he couldn't see it until it was too late."

"Was he alone in the car?"

"He was with his family coming back from a holiday in Queensland. None of them survived."

Just then, Jeff Bartrum the principal walked in with a big lady. "Good morning. I suppose that you all know by now what happened to Neil." He paused and looked around the room.

Jon locked eyes with the lady for a couple of seconds before she looked around the room.

"I would like to introduce Betty Willis who will be taking over Neil's duties. Betty?"

"Thank you, Jeff. I'm sure that you can all appreciate that to accept a position under these circumstances is not an easy thing to do, so I especially need your support to start with. From what I understand, Neil was an effective vice principal, but his way of doing things is a little different to mine."

"You can say that again," Jon sayed to Mark under his breath.

"During the day, I intend to meet each of you in turn to discuss what you are doing to further students' achievements, and to look for ways that you can do more. I want to see Hidey High become one of the best schools in the state, and I'm confident that if we all work together, we can achieve that goal. Thank you, Jeff."

"Thank you, Betty. And welcome. Right, I'm sure that you have a lot to discuss at your department meetings, so let's come back here after the morning break. We need to talk about strategies with our problem students, and I'm sure that Betty has some ideas."

"She has no idea," Jon sayed to Mark, again under his breath.

"Okay, let's go to our department meetings."

"It seems that you know her," Mark sayed as they goed out of the staff room.

"Yes, he does," Betty sayed from behind. "Jon, you're first."

"Sit down, Jon," she sayed when they entered the vice principal's office. "I'm rather surprised to see that you're teaching again. So how's it going?"

"A lot better at this school," Jon replied.

"All right, we had our differences at Kurropnagroopna, but let's put them behind us. Now, I understand that you replaced Maurice Hoare. Is that correct?"

"Yes, Betty. That's correct."

"Why did Neil make the replacement?"

"Because Maurice went on long service leave."

"Why did he go on long service leave?"

"I have no idea, Betty."

"All right, that's all that I need to know for now. Oh, just one more thing. You're on a contract now, right?"

"That's correct."

"When does it end?"

"The end of this year. Why do you ask?"

"No reason."

Ingrid decided not to accept Jon's suggestion to use standard English when it beed her turn to see Betty.

"Sit down, Ingrid. Now, you are the special English teacher. Is that correct?"

"Yes, Betty. That be correct."

"Tell me why it's necessary for this school to have a special English teacher."

"Because we have students who've recently arrived from other countries who ben't familiar with English."

"From what I've heard so far, it seems that you are not familiar with English."

"Here be what I've heared so far, Betty. You beed head of the English department at Kurropnagroopna High and you failed to support Jon when he haved problems with the students and their parents."

"We're here to discuss you – not Jon."

"Oh? What be there to discuss?"

"The way that you talk for a start."

"Be there any part of it that you don't understand?"

"That's not the point."

"Betty, as head of an English department, you must have realized that 'correct' English ben't necessary for communicating."

"Yes, Ingrid, I realize that. What you don't seem to realize is that students need to speak in line with the proper standards."

"You be right. I don't realize that. Have you looked at my records?"

"Briefly."

"And in your brief look, have you not noticed that within twelve months, every student that I've beed gived be able to communicate effectively?"

"By getting them to talk the way that you talk?"

"By letting them talk the way that I talk. Look, Betty, I've haved this conversation before with Neil, and if it be good enough for him to accept my approach, then it should be good enough for you."

"I see. All right, Ingrid, that's all for now. Tell Richard Tremayne that I want to see him."

"Tell me something, Betty. In what way be this interview supposed to further students' achievements?"

"Don't trust her as far as you can throw her," Jon said in Mark's office during the morning break. "She's the main reason why I quit teaching before."

"Be you thinking about quitting again?" Ingrid asked.

"I might be forced to."

"You cannot be fired, Jon – unless you do something criminal," Mark sayed. "It may be that your contract won't be extended."

"Which is the end of this year."

"Are you still interested in Korea?"

"Definitely."

"We may be on the same plane," Ingrid sayed.

At home the following evening, Jon settled down to the essays that beed handed in that day, and most beed about activities during the term break. YeongTae, however, haved writed about choices, and started out with:

*I speak the way that I want to speak, and that be my choice for
me. When I ben't at school or at home, I choose who I speak
with. Even at home, I choose to say as little as possible.*

Jon thought back to when he maked the same choice with his
parents.

*I choose not to go to my parents for advice. I learned a long
time ago when I beed in Korea that what happened when they
beed at school be different to what happen now.*

'Same for me,' Jon thought. 'Same for most people.'

*If I need advice, I ask a friend who I can trust. Or I go to a
teacher who I can trust. I know that I can trust my English
teacher. I can tell him things, and I know that he willn't tell
other teachers or anyone else in the school.*

'I got it, YeongTae. Don't worry. I'm ready when you are.
I just wish that Jody Greggs had as much trust.' Jon beed
about to put a circle around *willn't*, but decided not to. The
rest of the essay beed about the few friends at school, and
Jon seed that Hisham Moussa, also in 8C, beed one of them.
'Perhaps they should be sitting together.'

10

A few weeks more late on the Wednesday evening, Jon beed preparing a lesson when the phone ringed.

"Jon, this is your mother."

"Well, I didn't think that you're the Queen of England."

"Jon, for once in your life, can you be serious?"

"Certainly, Mother. What is there to be serious about?"

"Your grandmother passed away this afternoon."

"Oh, I'm sorry. When's the funeral?"

"Monday."

"Can it be Sunday?"

"Look, Jon, you missed out on your grandfather's funeral. Surely you can come to your grandmother's. Can't you do this for your father?"

"What about James? He stayed with her for a while when he left home, didn't he?"

"He has a business to run, Jon. You know that."

"Of course he has. Mother, I really don't see how my being there will make any difference."

"All right. Well … I assume that you will be here for the school holidays."

"Correct. Can I talk with Dad?"

"He's not well, Jon. He may not even be able to attend the funeral. That's why we want you here."

"Well, schedule it for Sunday, and I'll be there."

"It can't be changed, Jon."

"And I can't change my classes."

At morning break on the following day, Peter Jenkins comed to Jon's office. "Got a minute?" he asked. "I'll come straight to the point. Maurice is coming back on Monday, and he will be taking his classes back. You'll be in the library."

"I see. When was this decision made?"

"I don't know. I was only told about it this morning."

"Isn't this your decision to make, Peter?"

"Well, normally, yes."

"So why didn't you normally make it?"

"Look, it doesn't matter whose decision it is."

"So you are comfortable with this, are you? What happens with YeongTae?"

"What do you mean?"

"Neil was about to make special arrangements for him before Maurice walked out of the school. You know that."

"Yeah, well …"

"Surely you can make a decision about that."

"It's not that easy."

"Do you mean that it's not that easy for you to make a decision?"

"Come on, Jon. That's not what I mean."

"Then what do you mean?"

"That it's not just my decision."

"That's what I thought," Jon sayed as he standed up.

"I wouldn't go and see her."

"That's for me to decide, Peter."

"I'm really busy right now," Betty sayed when Jon knocked at her door. "Perhaps you could come back later."

"This will only take a couple of minutes. Now that Maurice is returning to the classes that I have and I'm in the library, I would like you to consider YeongTae Kim having his English classes in the library."

"Oh, nothing doing, Jon."

"Why not?"

"Well, for a start, he needs to be graded properly. You've been giving him A's for badly written essays."

"Who says that they are badly written?"

"Does he use standard English when he writes them?"

"Not exactly, but …"

"Then they are badly written."

"Betty, he is creative, he has a great imagination, and he is brilliant in the way that he expresses ideas. He has the potential to be a great writer, and Maurice will do nothing to further that potential."

"Jon, why do you have this special interest in YeongTae Kim? Now, I have a lot of things to do. Please close the door on your way out."

No more soon haved Jon sitted down in his office, Betty entered without knocking. "I understand that you have essays to hand back to the 8C students."

"Well, yes, but …"

"I'd like to see them."

"Why?"

"Because I'd like to see them."

"Why do you want to see them?"

Betty's response beed a cold, hard stare.

"A vice principal wanting to see essays written for an English class: this is highly unusual, don't you think? The answer is no, Betty. You're not seeing them."

"Then I'm relieving you of your duties until further notice."

"You're joking."

"I'm not joking. Until you show me those essays, you are relieved of your duties."

"You're a joke, Betty."

"Pack your things and leave the school, Jon."

"You're a bloody joke. The only way that you can get me to leave the school is to fire me – which you can't do. Now, you have a lot of things to do, and so have I. Please close the door on your way out."

The whole school heared it.

Jon locked the door and looked again at what YeongTae haved writed.

In any urban center in Korea, there be lots of shops, restaurants, offices, churches, and private schools. The shops and restaurants be usually at street level, and the offices, the more small churches, and the private schools be above them. These churches often put red crosses up high, and when they light up at night, they almost scream at each other.

Nearly every middle and high school student go to private schools after their regular school classes. A parent who don't send their kids to a private school be talked about by the neighbors as being a bad parent. Most of them be expensive, and most of the kids don't want to be there.

One of my teachers comed from Canada, and after three months, she refused to teach until she getted payed. Because she beed the only native speaker there, they doed pay. But it beed only a part of what she should have beed payed, so she refused to teach until she getted the rest of it. So she beed fired, and a Korean-American taked over her classes. The school closed down for good at the end of that month, and my brothers and I beed sended to another private school which also ripped off their teachers.

There be little street crime in Korea. It seem that most of the criminals run private schools.

It would have beed criminal not to give YeongTae an A for that essay.

There beed twenty minutes before the start of the next period, and Jon putted the essays into his bag and taked them with him to the principal's office. He beedn't surprised that Jeff beedn't there so he goed to the school office.

"Do you know when Jeff will be back?" he asked the school secretary.

"He had a meeting at the department of education this morning, so he should be back by now," Jenny Andrews sayed. "Let me guess: you have issues with Betty."

"However did you guess?"

"Ah, just a feeling. Well, if you want to wait for him, it may be better to wait in here. Ah, here he is."

Jon knocked at the door between Jeff's office and the secretary's office. "I'm sorry to trouble you, Jeff. I guess that you have a lot of things to attend to right now."

"Yes, I do, Jon, but one more thing is not going to make a lot of difference. So, what's happening with you?"

"My grandmother died yesterday, and the funeral service is on Monday."

"I'm sorry to hear that, Jon. If you need time off, we can cover your classes."

"What classes? Starting Monday, I'll have library duties. I was informed this morning that Maurice will have his classes back again on Monday."

"Like hell he will! Jenny, can you tell Betty that I want to see her in my office right now? Jon, how long do you want off on Monday?"

"The day. The funeral is in Melbourne."

"That shouldn't be a problem."

"Would Maurice be taking my classes?"

"Most likely."

"Then I prefer to stay here."

"Go to the funeral, Jon. That's an order."

"No, Jeff. I wasn't close to her at all."

"Your choice, Jon."

Just then, Betty appeared. "What's this about, Jeff? Oh, I see. You've decided to go over my head, have you, Jon?"

Jeff sitted back and watched Betty and Jon go into full flight. When they landed, "Well, I've learned quite a few things in the last five minutes – most of which I should have known before, Betty. Jon, you are continuing with your classes until the end of the year."

"Thank you, Jeff."

"There's no need to thank me. Can you close the door on your way out? Betty, can you close the other two doors before you sit down?"

"Jeff, I …"

Jeff getted up and closed the doors himself. "I think that you better sit down, Betty. I'm not going to tell you again."

Betty doed so.

"Betty, you were appointed to this school to work with me, not against me. Maurice and Richard are dead wood in this school, and yet you want Maurice to replace Jon? Why?"

"Because Jon is giving his students higher grades than what they deserve."

"Really? From what I just heard, you have no evidence to support that claim. None. And yet, you had already decided to take Jon off those classes without saying anything to me. Have you bothered to check the records of our past students?"

"I've had no time for that."

"Well, if you had've found time, you would have seen that all but a few of them have got lower grades in Maurice's and Richard's classes than in their other English classes. Also, are you aware that Maurice caused an incident with YeongTae Kim last term which he then couldn't handle?"

"Well, I don't know the exact details."

"Are you aware that Neil was going to make special arrangements for YeongTae? And that YeongTae's parents were in agreement?"

"I heard something about it."

"And?"

"And what?"

"Did you follow it up? Betty, are there any other fires that you've started around the school that I have to put out? Here's the deal: from here on in, any matters that concern teachers and parents will be handled by me. Not you. Your job now is to handle student discipline. Just that. Do you understand me?"

"Is it true that Mr. Hoare will be taking this class again on Monday?" Jon beed asked when handing back the essays.

"No, it's not true. I'm afraid that you're stuck with me for the rest of the year."

That evening, as Jon beed preparing a lesson, the phone ringed. 'No, Mother. I won't be at the funeral if it's on Monday.'

"Jon, it's Brent. I should have told you before, but Jody has a job. He's working in a soft drink factory."

"I hope that he's not drinking the profits."

"I doubt it. He would have been fired by now if he was. Listen, what I really called about is that he finally opened up about what happened last year. Question: did anyone notice that he and the head of the English department missed school on the same day?"

"They did? Yeah, come to think of it, that's right. I should have realized. As far as I know, no one noticed. So is this a police matter?"

"It is. We've just got back from the police station, and they're going to arrest the woman tonight."

"Betty Willis."

"That's the one. She gave you a hard time at Kurropnagroopna, didn't she?"

"She's still giving me a hard time. She's now the vice principal at Hidey High."

"Well, she won't be tomorrow. Do you want to talk with Jody?"

"Yeah, sure. Put him on. Jody?"

"Hi, Jon. I just want to say thank you for still believing in me."

"That's easy, Jody. So, where to now?"

"Just put the past behind me and move on."

"Yeah. Keep in touch, eh?"

"Are you coming to Melbourne during the next holidays?"

"Sure. And I plan to stay with you and Brent – if you don't mind sleeping in the living room for a couple of weeks."

First thing the next morning, Jeff called a meeting in the staff room. "I suppose that some of you are aware that we've just lost our second vice principal this year. She was arrested last night for an incident with a year ten student at Kurropnagroopna High last year. Look, I'm sure that I don't need to say this, but if any of you notice a change in a student's behavior, even a small change, then I want to know about it. Now, we need yet another vice principal, and I would prefer to put forward someone from this school. I want to do that this afternoon, so if anyone is interested, let me know before lunch. Are there any questions?"

"Maybe Maurice Hoare could take the job," comed from the back.

"Out of the question. Next?"

Mark putted up his hand. "I gather that you don't want to bring in someone from outside to replace whoever takes the job."

"Exactly."

"So that would mean that the next vice principal needs to come from the English department."

"True. Does anyone have any problems with that?"

"I do. At the risk of sounding personal, it means that Maurice would replace that person, and I'm not sure that it's a good idea."

"What we do in the English department is none of your bloody business, Mark!" Richard called out from the side.

Mark standed up and stared at Richard.

"Gentlemen, please," Jeff sayed.

Mark sitted down still staring at Richard.

"Look, here's the situation. I think that you're all aware that teachers' salaries are paid out of the school budget, and therefore, if we have to bring another teacher in, that's less money for other things. I'm afraid that Maurice will have to take over the classes of whoever becomes the vice principal. Whoever is interested in the job please come and see me before lunch."

"Whoever want to abandon their classes," Ingrid sayed under her breath.

"I'm really not interested," Peter sayed to Jeff at the end of the morning break. "I think that it's important for me to stay as head of department."

"Is that the only thing?"

"Jeff, you know that I cannot leave any of my students to be taught by Maurice. And most of the other teachers feel the same way. Did Richard come and see you?"

"He did."

"Give him the job."

"Are you serious? Richard couldn't organize a drink in a pub."

"So make him an acting vice principal. When he messes up, you should be able to replace him and get him transferred to another school. I'm willing to cover for his mistakes, and I'm sure that Mark and the other heads of department would also be willing."

"That's not a bad strategy, Peter. Not bad at all."

"Perhaps we could put Maurice in there."

"That would be better, but the trouble is that I have to get this approved by the education officials. I think that I've got a better chance by putting Richard's name forward."

"So what happens when you have to tell the officials that you made a mistake?"

"Everyone makes mistakes, Peter."

On Monday evening, Jon getted a call that he should have expected. "Good evening, Mother. How was the funeral?"

"You should have been here to find out."

"Well, I'm sorry about that."

"So you bloody well should be. I needed you here, Jon."

"Why? Just to show myself?"

"Because I had to take your father to the hospital, and then rush to the funeral. I had to give the speech, Jon. That was your job."

"Or James's."

"You know that he couldn't be here."

"And you know that I couldn't be there."

"Jon, he has a business to run, and Perth is a long way away from Melbourne."

"And therefore, he is in a much better position to organize his schedule to make the trip across. The schedule that I have is set and cannot be changed just for me. Do you know what would have been easier to change? The day of the funeral. Anyway, how's Dad?"

"He's not well, Jon. Are you still thinking of coming to Melbourne for the next break?"

"Of course."

"Even though you weren't here today."

"Where are we going with this, Mother?"

"Jon, you don't seem to realize the strain that I'm under. If you think that it's easy to manage this house by myself, and go and attend to your father, you have another thing coming?"

"Another think coming."

"All right, Mr. English Teacher. You're not in the classroom now. The point is that I have far too much work to do, and I haven't got time to wait on you hand and foot."

"You won't have to. I'm quite able to take care of myself."

"That's not what I saw before."

"That's because you didn't give me a chance. Or my wife. You just came in and took over everything."

"Another thing: your father is a very sick man, and he doesn't need any of your diseases."

"I don't have any. You're the one who gets heavy colds every winter. How often have you seen me with a cold?"

"I've lost count, Jon."

"There are none to count. If anyone should be with Dad, it's me."

"Well, I can't stop you from coming, but if you come here and kill him, there'll be hell to pay. Do you understand me?"

"The only thing that I understand right now is that you don't want to see me, and that you don't want my father to see me. Fine. You win."

The following evening, there beed another call from Melbourne.

"How do you feel, Jon?"

"Oh, absolutely wonderful, Mother. Top of the world."

"You can see my point, can't you?"

"Not at all."

"Jon, be reasonable."

"How the hell can I reason with you? You've made it clear that you don't want to see me, and you won't."

"Jon, I …"

He haved cutted the call, and leaved the phone off the hook until he getted up the next morning.

Just as he beed heading out the door, the phone ringed. He stopped, looked at it for about half a minute, and leaved.

Toward the end of term, Mark beed called to Jeff's office. "I have two matters that you can help me with," Jeff sayed. "I suppose that you know that Maurice is having discipline problems with his classes."

"Everyone knows, Jeff."

"He's thinking of quitting."

"Well, you don't need my help with that."

"Actually, I do. I understand that you have contacts in Korea."

"I do, but not for Maurice. My contacts are important to me."

"Look, I don't want to put pressure on you, but the only way that he will quit is if he has somewhere to go."

"And there's nowhere in Australia for him to go?"

"Exactly."

"What's the other matter, Jeff?"

"I suppose that you know that Richard is not managing the vice principal's job too well."

"Again, everyone knows, Jeff. What, do you want me to find a job in Korea for him as well?"

"No. He can get transferred to another school. I'm wondering if you are interested in taking over his job. I'm talking about on a permanent basis."

"Shouldn't you now be considering a female for the job?"

"Mark, we both know that equal opportunity is a joke, and so do the people at the department of education, or they should by now – especially after what happened with Betty Willis. Of course, no one can say this in public. Mark, I don't care if you have to wear a dress and make your chest look bigger, I want to work with you."

"Even without that, I belong in the classroom, Jeff."

"So do I. I would much rather be teaching than running from meeting to meeting. Speaking of which, I'm going to another one this morning, and I would like to put your name forward. Look, I don't want to put pressure on you, Mark, but it's either you or someone from another school."

"That's two things that you are pressuring me on."

Jeff gave a weak smile. "Sorry."

Mark hesitated. "Okay. I'll take the vice principal's job, but I need an experienced teacher to take over my classes. Not some kid fresh out of teachers college. And who's available at this time of year?"

"There are plenty of teachers on the other side of the Blue Mountains who would jump at the chance to move back to Sydney. Thanks, Mark. Let's see if my recommendation is accepted. So, can you do something for Maurice? Today?"

"Jeff tells me that you're thinking about teaching in Korea," Mark sayed as he entered Maurice's office.

"That's right. I was wondering if you could give me a few contacts. It would make things a lot easier for me."

"I'm sure that it would – until you get there."

"What do you mean?"

"Your teaching style is not suitable for the positions that are available to you."

"I can adapt."

"Just like you've adapted to the new approaches to teaching here. Maurice, if you want a job in another country, check the newspaper."

That evening, Jon rolled his eyes as he picked up the phone. 'I said that I'm not coming, Mother dear.'

"Good evening, Jon."

"Dad! How are you doing?"

"Not too well, to be honest. What's this that I hear about you not coming to Melbourne?"

"That's your loving wife's choice, Dad."

"I want you here."

"She doesn't."

"Look, don't take any notice of your mother. So, can you be here or not?"

"Well, I can, but …"

"Thank you. We have a bed for you this time."

"I would rather stay in Collingwood."

"I would much rather that you stay here."

"Sorry, Dad. I'll stay in Collingwood."

"All right, if that's the way that you feel. Get down here as soon as you can."

"Thanks, Mark," Jeff sayed the following week.

"For what?"

"Finding Maurice a job in Korea."

"I didn't find him a job. I just told him to check the newspaper. So where's he going?"

"Seoul."

"A university?"

"That's right." Jeff gived the name of the university.

"Oh, hell. I have a contact there. Or I did."

11

On the last day of the second term, Jon rushed home as soon as he could, throwed a couple of bags into the car, maked sure that everything beed turned off, and locked up before driving off. This time, he needed to be alone, even though the journey beed over 900 kilometers.

After a few light taps on the front door in the small hours of Saturday morning, "Jody's already asleep," Brent sayed. "Do you mind sleeping in the living room? I'll see you in a few hours."

Over breakfast, Jon noticed that Jody haved filled out a bit. "Have they been working you hard, Jody?"

"Yeah, but it's better than going to a health center," he replied.

"Listen, Jon," Brent sayed, "I have to work today. Why don't you call your parents now?"

"Where are you now?" Andrea asked.

"In Collingwood," Jon replied.

"Jon, your father's back in hospital."

"When did that happen?"

"On Wednesday."

"Don't you think that you should have let me know?"

"Jon, you have no idea of how busy I am."

"Well, Mother, do you think that you could possibly spare a moment to inform me of which hospital he's in?"

"What? Are you going to visit him?"

"No, Mother. I'm going to go there and paint the west wall before the sun sets."

"I hope that you haven't got any diseases."

"Just Purple Pizza Disease, Mother. I'll try not to pass it on."

"Jon, when are you going to learn to be serious?"

"When I learn of what hospital Dad is in."

"He's in Collingwood District Hospital."

"Thank you. I don't suppose that he has a phone in his room."

"Jon, we really have to get going," Brent sayed.

"Who's that?" Andrea asked.

"Do you have his number?" Jon asked.

"Well, I'll have to look for it."

"Don't bother." Jon hanged up the phone. "Let's go. Can you tell me where Collingwood District Hospital is?"

"Oh, that's just down the street from the record shop," Brent sayed. "Let's go together."

"I've come to see Joseph Mamjjasond," Jon sayed at the reception desk.

"Oh, you must be his son," the nurse sayed.

"That's correct. I believe that he's expecting me."

"Well, yes, but not until tomorrow. You must've got an early flight."

"I drove."

"From Perth?"

"From Sydney. I'm Jon Mamjjasond."

"Oh. Not James."

"No, not James. He's my older brother."

"And you are?"

"Jon."

"Just a minute." She picked up the phone and pressed three times. "Mr. Mamjjasond, there's Jon to see you. ... Certainly." She hanged up the phone. "You'll find him in room 12A. Upstairs to the first floor, turn right, down the passage, and it's on the left."

Jon found 12A between rooms 12 and 14. Although the door beed open, Jon knocked. Joe moved his hand a little, and Jon goed in and standed next to the bed.

"You're allowed to sit down," Joe sayed. "That's why they provide chairs in here."

Jon pulled up a chair and sitted down. "How are you feeling, Dad?"

"I'm in a hospital, Jon. How do you think I feel? Have you seen your mother yet?"

"I've only spoken with her on the phone."

"I assume that you will be staying at our house while you're here."

"I would rather stay in Collingwood."

"Jon, there have been a few forced entries in the street recently, and I'm worried about your mother being there alone. I want you there."

"Why not James?"

"You know as well as I do that James and your mother do not get along."

"Nor do I."

"Look, Jon, I really don't want to argue about this. I want somebody in that house during the night. Can you be there or not?"

"Well, yes. I suppose."

"Thank you. Now what's happening with teaching?"

"I'm happy. The principal and the other teachers are easy to work with, and the kids are great. And we're getting yet another vice principal at the start of this term, and he's also great."

"Yet another?"

"It's a long story, Dad. Are you really interested?"

"Not really. Anyway, I'm glad that you're back in teaching. Is there any way that you can become permanent again?"

"I doubt it."

"Well, you burned that bridge when you quit before."

"I know that, Dad. You don't have to tell me."

Just then, Andrea appeared. "How are you feeling, Joe?" she asked as she sitted in the chair on the other side of the bed.

"I'm not good, Andrea. Listen, James will be here tomorrow, so I want you two here as well."

"When was that arranged?"

"Last night."

"And where will he be staying?"

"In a hotel close by. Don't worry, he can claim it as a tax expense."

"And where will you be staying, Jon?"

"He's staying in our house."

"Don't I get a say in this?"

"Oh, don't start, Andrea. We discussed this before."

"Right, Jon, you can stay, but you better pull your weight around the place. I'm not running a hotel."

"I know that," Jon replied. "Look, Mother, if you don't want me there ..."

"Jon, I want you in the house," Joe sayed. "Haven't I made that clear to you yet?"

"You've both made it clear what each of you want. As it's not the same thing, I think that I get the deciding vote."

Joe breathed out heavily. "All right, Jon. You make your choice. If this guy in Collingwood is more important to you than we are, then go and stay with him. What's the phone number there?"

"What's the number here?"

"Have a look. It's on the phone."

Jon smiled when he seed that the last two figures beed 13.

"Right. Your mother and I have things to talk about. Call me in the morning to see what time that I want you here."

Jon beed waiting near the reception desk when Andrea comed out of the elevator. "You're not ill," he sayed.

"What are you talking about?"

"I'm talking about the sign that says that the elevator is only for the use of patients, doctors, nurses, and other hospital staff. Unless there is something that I'm not aware of, you don't fit into any of those categories."

"So why are you here, Jon? To check on me?"

"I want to ask you if you want me to stay in the house."

"That's up to you, Jon. If you want …"

"Mother, I'm asking what you want."

"All right, you can stay at the house, Jon, but one argument – just one – and you're out. Am I making myself clear?"

"Clear as a bell, Mother."

Jon choosed to park in the street and to let Andrea park in the drive.

"Now, you can see that there's a lot of work to be done around here," Andrea sayed as they entered the house.

"You're not wrong, Mother."

"Well, you better get started. I want the grass cut before lunch, and then you can start on the garden."

"Your wish is my command, Mother. Would you like the house raised a few centimeters before dinner?"

"What I'd like to see raised, Jon, is the level of your intelligence."

With the sky clouding over and the air smelling fresh, Jon wasted no time with starting on the grass. Just before he finished, rain started to fall, and by the time that he putted things away, it beed heavy. He beed wet through when he standed at the back door.

"I suppose that you want to have a shower," Andrea sayed from inside.

"That would be nothing short of wonderful, Mother. Is there any chance of taking off my clothes in the bathroom? I'll attend to the passage when I'm warm again." A few minutes after he entered the bathroom, he beed out again with a towel around him. "Would you mind turning on the hot water?"

"I've turned it on. You just need to let it run for a while."

"Indeed I did. All right, let me check the switch at the front."

"I've turned it on, Jon. Half an hour ago. Anyway, lunch is almost ready."

After about ten minutes, Jon appeared in the kitchen with many clothes on. "Well, it looks like I have another job this afternoon. I wasn't really interested in attending to the garden anyway."

"What are you talking about?"

"I just had a cold shower."

"You probably didn't have the taps set properly."

"You really do have doubts about my intelligence level, don't you?"

"Jon, it was working all right yesterday."

"So it might have been, but it isn't now. I'll check the wiring after lunch."

"What do you know about electricity?"

"I probably know more about electrical wiring than anyone else in the family."

"Well, I hope that you don't mind egg and chicken sandwiches."

"Chicken in both the early and late stages of development combined together. It sounds a real treat."

"Do you want them or not?"

"What else is there?"

"Whatever you can find."

"Egg and chicken is fine, Mother. No salt."

"I've already put salt on. Do you want coffee or tea? Oh, we've just run out of coffee."

"Ah, so I can choose between tea and tea. Ooh. This is difficult. Okay, I'll have … tea. No milk. I'll add my own sugar."

"One day, you will say something intelligent."

"And you won't even know when it happens."

After a while: "Jon, how often do you get in touch with James?"

"About the same number of times that he gets in touch with me."

"Which is what?"

"The only number that you cannot divide by."

"Which is?"

"Think back to your school days, Mother."

"So you're a maths teacher now."

"No. Most people remember that you cannot divide by zero. How often are you and James in touch?"

"He's often in touch with your father. Jon, tell me about your friend in Collingwood."

"What do you want to know?"

"Is he gay?"

Jon putted down his sandwich. "Now I understand." He standed up. "I should have bloody known."

"Jon, sit down. No one is accusing you."

"Then why did you ask me if my friend in Collingwood is gay?"

"We're concerned about you, Jon."

"So I noticed. When you see James tomorrow, tell him that when he wants to talk about me, he should talk to me."

"You can tell him yourself."

"I'll be on my way back to Sydney."

"So you're abandoning us."

"Isn't that what this family wants?"

There beed no one else in the record shop while Jon telled what happened.

"Jon, if you were gay, we would have been partners long ago," Brent sayed. "So what are you going to do?"

"I'm going back to Sydney, but I need a good night's sleep before I start driving."

"Of course. Here's a key. I'll see you at around seven. Jody should be home before then. You're too tired even to be walking around the neighborhood. I'll wake you up when it's time for dinner."

The dream that Jon waked with beed a friendly fight with both Brent and Jody where they beed pushing one another, and Brent haved pushed him hard enough that he falled onto the bed. When he opened his eyes, Brent beed standing over him pushing him on the shoulder. "Dinner's ready, Jon."

It taked Jon almost five minutes to move from the second bedroom into the kitchen and collapse into a chair in front of a plate of steak and vegetables. "You didn't have to go to this much trouble, Brent."

"Well, after having chicken and egg for lunch, I didn't think that you would want steak and milk for dinner. Well, two, four, six, eight. Dig in; don't wait." As they beed eating: "Are you still heading home to Sydney, Jon?"

"Exactly."

"When?"

"First thing in the morning – if that's okay with you."

"Jon, why don't you stay here for your holiday break?" Jody asked.

"You know that you're welcome," Brent sayed. "Look, you know your situation better than anyone else, but from what you've told me, you've done everything right for your family. Why stop now?"

"Brent, I ..."

"Jon, if they think that you're gay, you're not going to be able to change their minds, especially if you cut yourself off from them now. Anyway, perhaps I've said too much."

"No, you haven't, Brent. You haven't."

"I heard about your performance this afternoon," Joe sayed when Jon called him after dinner. "Are you in Sydney yet?"

"I'm still in Melbourne, Dad. In Collingwood. Do you want the number?"

"Is there any point?"

"It's 4-1-7 ..."

"Just wait a minute. All right. 4-1-7. What's the rest of it?"

Jon gave the remaining four numbers and Joe repeated them.

"So I take it that you can be here tomorrow morning. When can you make it?"

"Whenever you want. Six?"

"Well, that's a bit early. How about 8:30?"

"I'm expecting your mother and brother to be here soon, and I want you here," Joe sayed the next morning. "Now, are you staying in Melbourne for the next two weeks?"

"Yes, I am."

"In Collingwood."

"Yes."

"Jon, what I said before still applies. I want you to stay with your mother while you're here."

"I don't."

"Jon, can't you put aside …"

"Have you asked James?"

"All right. If that's how you feel."

Jon paused. "Dad, I know that you prefer to believe James more than me, but I'm going to say this anyway. I'm not gay. Never have been; never will be."

"Okay."

"What else has James been saying about me?"

"It's not important. Look, Jon …"

"Dad, the next time that he wants to talk about me, tell him to call me and say it."

"You can tell him that yourself."

"When he arrives? Do you really think that it's a good idea?"

"Well, it's up to you."

Just then, James arrived. "How are you feeling, Dad?"

"He's in a hospital, James. How do you think he feels?"

James looked at Jon, and turned back to Joe. "How badly are you feeling, Dad?"

"I'll talk about that when your mother arrives. My main concern right now is you two. I know that brothers don't always get on, but I would like to see you two get on better than what I've just seen."

"Yes, it might help when one of us has got something to say about the other, he says it to the other first."

"What the hell are you talking about?" James asked.

"Tell him, Dad. I'll be back in five minutes."

After Jon left the room: "I'm afraid that your mother's tongue has become a little loose recently. Anyway, how's your business going?"

"Fine. I've got good staff, and while I'm away …"

"Yet you couldn't attend your grandmothers' and grandfather's funerals."

"Did Jon?"

"All right. I get the idea. Asking you two to behave more like brothers is like talking to a brick wall."

"Dad, Jon has his life, and I have mine. What am I supposed to do?"

"Just handle our wills fairly. That's all I ask."

They beed in silence until Jon returned with Andrea. "Sit down, Mother. James, as you are older than I am, you can have the other chair. I feel that it's proper that I stand." Jon standed at the foot of the bed.

"All right," Joe started, "now that you're all here, there are some things that I must make clear to you. To answer your question, James, I'm in more pain than ever before. I don't sleep well, the smallest sound causes pain, and my many requests to reduce the amount of light in this room have been ignored."

"I'll talk to them," James sayed.

"Leave it, James. It will just cause trouble, and that's the last thing that I want. I want to ask you all a question, and I want you to think about it seriously. Should I consider quality of life over quantity of life, or the other way round?"

No one speaked.

"Jon? What do you think?"

"Dad, this is the first time ever that you've asked me a question like this."

"What's your answer?"

"I have no answer, Dad. Only you can answer that."

"James?"

"I'm afraid that I have to agree with Jon."

"Andrea?"

"Jon's right. You have to answer that question for yourself."

Just then, a doctor appeared. "Can you give me a few minutes with Joe?"

"You want us to leave?" James asked.

"That's the idea. Please close the door behind you."

"James, remember what I said," Joe sayed.

Out in the passage, the three looked through the window until the blind beed pulled down.

"Why did he ask us about quality and quantity?" James asked. "He has always been more willing to tell us what we should be doing with our lives."

"And did you take any notice of him? Either of you?" Andrea asked. "Of course not. Both of you just did what you wanted to do without thinking about anyone else."

"Mother, this is not a good time."

"Isn't it? When is a good time, James? You never want to talk with me when you call; you only want to talk with your father."

"That's my choice, Mother."

"Just like it was your choice to leave home when you were 16 and just abandon us?"

"Who abandoned us when I was 14?" Jon asked.

"Stay out of this, Jon."

"No, Mother, I won't. It's you who does whatever you want to do without thinking about anyone else."

"Is that right? After all the things that I've done for you, and you have the nerve to tell me that."

"Done for us? Like the way that you got James into trouble for things that he never did? Like the way that you ruined my marriage?"

"You can't blame me for that."

"Oh, yes, but I can. I would probably be still married now if you hadn't decided to abandon Dad when he moved down here, and impose yourself on Rachel and me in Kurropnagroopna."

"Jon ..."

Just then, the doctor comed out. "You can go back in there now."

When they entered the room, "Well, what a wonderful performance that you three put on out there," Joe sayed. "Now that the whole bloody hospital has started to hear about our private affairs, you should have stayed out there and finished it off."

"Dad," Jon started.

"No, Jon. You've said quite enough for one day. Let me clear up one thing right now. I have never told any of you what you should do with your lives. I've made suggestions, but I never gave advice. I've never stood in anyone's way – even when you decided to leave home when you were 16, James."

"I know, Dad," James sayed.

"And I think that you should have," Andrea sayed.

"Andrea, we all know why James made that decision. And don't tell me that I brought it about. Now, let's change the subject. Do either of you two have anything to tell me?"

James and Jon looked at each other before they shaked their heads.

"Then I'll see you tomorrow. Andrea, we need to talk."

"Let's get some coffee," James sayed to Jon on the way out.

"Andrea, I really don't understand you. When the hell are you going to take responsibility for the things that you've done?"

"What are you talking about?" she replied.

"You know exactly what I'm talking about. You've told me several times that Jon is gay, and it's something that I keep hearing from James. Tell me something, Andrea: why do you think that he's gay?"

"I've given you my reasons, and you've agreed with them."

"Yes. Yes, I did. Andrea, I need time alone. See you tomorrow."

Down in the coffee shop: "How's teaching, Jon?"

"Great. Much better than before."

"You know, our father has often told me that he's proud of you."

"He has never said that to me. This is what gets me about our family. You and our parents are quite happy to talk about me, but never to me. Let me make one thing clear to you, not that it's any of your bloody business. I am not gay."

"I never said that you are. Who told you that I said that?"

"Guess. No, don't bother. Here she is."

"Well, it's good to see you again, Jon. Keep in touch." James standed.

"Sit down, James," Andrea commanded.

"I can't, Mother dear. I have a lot of phone calls to make."

"James, I want to …"

"I've got to go. You can finish off my coffee if you like."

To Jon's horror, his mother picked up the coffee cup as she sitted down. "So what were you two talking about?"

"That he never said that I'm gay."

"Oh, that's not true, Jon. He has often said that to your father."

"How do you know?"

"Your father has told me."

"There's something that I don't quite understand here, so help me out. James has often said that to Dad, and Dad has told you each time. Have I got that right?"

"Yes. What's your point?"

"Why is this being often said? Isn't once enough? You can have the rest of my coffee too." Jon getted up and walked out.

12

The next morning, Jon arrived at the hospital at 8:30 with a list of questions in mind for his father before his mother showed up. When he getted to the room, it beed empty.

"Excuse me," Nurse Morris sayed. "Who do you want to see?"

"The man who was in here yesterday and several days before."

"And you are?"

"His younger son."

"Can I have your name, please?"

"Excuse me?"

"Your name, please."

"Jon Mamjjasond. My father is Joe Mamjjasond."

"Can you come this way, please?"

"I would rather see my father first."

"Please come this way. This won't take long." In a small office: "Can I have your father's full name?"

"Why?"

"Please give it to me."

"Joseph Francis Mamjjasond. Two J's in Mamjjasond."

"And I need your full name."

"Jonathan Frederick Mamjjasond."

"Thank you. I'm sorry to have to tell you this, but your father died this morning at 1:37. Were you not informed?"

"No, ma'am. I wasn't."

"That's strange. Let me check on this. It may take a while."

"Can I see my father?"

"Yes, of course. It will take about ten minutes. Can I leave you in here?"

"Certainly."

When the nurse closed the door, Jon standed and looked at the charts on the wall. There beed nothing of interest, so he sitted again.

After a few minutes, he beed about to stand and walk out when the nurse opened the door. "Mr. Mamjjasond – can I call you Jon?"

"Sure."

"You can call me Bev. The reason why you weren't contacted is because we don't have a phone number for you."

"I gave it to my father."

"Apparently the night staff didn't see it."

"But they contacted my mother and brother."

"Yes, they did."

"So why didn't they ask … No, don't worry."

"What?"

"They don't have my number. But I have another question. Why did you ask me all those questions to find out who I am?"

"Oh, we have to do that."

"Because you didn't know who I am?"

"That's right."

"Yet I made myself known on Saturday morning. Apparently, they didn't know about me before that."

"Well, Jon, I can only apologize. Okay, you can go and view your father's body now. Please come this way. Jon?"

"Will I be alone with him?"

"Of course."

"Then it's better that I don't see him. And I apologize for any trouble that I may have caused." Jon getted up.

"Do you want to leave your number?"

"It's not necessary now. If you happen to find it, please don't give it to anyone, especially my mother and brother. Please."

"Are you all right?"

"No, Bev. I can't believe what happened, and what didn't happen."

"Do you have anyone who you can talk with?"

"Yes, I do, Bev."

"You're lucky, Jon," Brent sayed in the record shop. "I normally have a lot of people in here at this time. So, what's the latest development?"

"My father's dead."

"Oh, hell! I'm sorry. I'm so sorry."

"Don't be."

"Oh, come on. Don't be like that."

"I am like that, and with good reason. Look, can I …"

"Jon, you're free to come and go as you please."

"Thanks. Tell you what. Let me prepare the dinner for this evening."

"You don't have to."

"Don't worry. It won't be chicken and egg sandwiches. Please, I need something to do this afternoon or I'll go crazy."

"Sure. Surprise me."

Within five minutes of Jon arriving at Brent's, the phone ringed. He looked at it for about half a minute before he picked it up. He beed about to say, 'Brent's phone,' but it beed "Good afternoon" instead.

"It's Bev Morris here. Can I talk with Jon Mamjjasond?"

"This is Jon."

"Jon, we found this number …"

"Obviously."

"Well, yes, right, and your mother is insisting on having it. She's here with me now."

"Have you given it to her?"

"No. You said not to."

"Oh, thank you. I would like you to destroy it. This is not my phone. Can I speak with her?"

"It will have to be brief."

"Don't worry. It will be."

Andrea comed on the phone. "Jon?"

"When will you be home, Mother?"

"I cannot be sure."

"I'll call you at three." Jon hanged up.

"This is great," Brent sayed over dinner. "How long did you take to prepare this?"

"Not that long, really."

"Oh, come on. This must have taken you all afternoon."

"No, not at all. Actually, I spent more time with the shopping." 'And on the phone. Local call.'

"You must give me the recipe."

"Sure. I've written it out already."

"Oh, you're wonderful."

"Thanks, Brent. I'm glad that someone thinks so."

"We both think so. Right, Jody?"

"Absolutely," Jody replied. "If it wasn't for you, I don't know where I'd be now."

"You are going to the funeral."

Jon breathed out heavily.

"Come on, Jon. You've got to go. Not many people have a second funeral. You're going, Jon, even if we have to take time off work and drag you there kicking and screaming. When is it?"

"Thursday at ten."

"Perhaps I should be there. I'd love to see a bit of blood."

"It might be yours."

"Not a chance. You haven't seen me in action."

"Nor me," Jody added.

James's speech at the funeral service beed without any notes, whereas Jon haved something prepared. They focused on their father's good points, and so James taked more time than Jon. Minutes after the service, James beed in a taxi on his way to the airport.

'No doubt another tax write-off,' Jon thought to himself. He looked at his mother. "Are you okay?"

"I would be if you could be a little more help."

"In what way?"

"Oh, forget it, Jon."

"How about telling me how I can be of more help?"

"Do you really want to know?"

"Yes, I do."

"Well, there are lots of things to be done around the house."

"Any other way?"

"Somebody to walk the dog."

"You have a dog?"

"Not yet."

"How else?"

"I'd like to have somebody around in case I need to be rushed to hospital."

"Mother, I'm teaching in Sydney, remember?"

"Can't you transfer down to Melbourne?"

"No, not while the government here is closing down schools. You're right about lots of things that need to be done around the house, but I haven't the skills or the tools to do them. Perhaps you should consider a retirement village."

"All right, Jon. I didn't think that you're willing to help. Off you go. Don't worry about me. I'll survive for a few more years yet. Alone."

"I'm sorry that I couldn't talk with you in the record shop today," Brent sayed that evening over another of Jon's cooking delights.

"No problem. You had quite a crowd in there."

"That's what I usually have. So, how did it go?"

"The funeral service was fine. Straight after it, James rushed off to the airport at half the speed of light, leaving me with Mother."

"So, I suppose that you want to head back to Sydney tomorrow."

"Not at all. Mother has my number in Sydney. I'd like to stay here for as long as I can – if that's okay with you two."

"That's fine. You're the best cook that I've ever come across."

13

"I've just got back, Mother. The reason why you couldn't leave any more messages on the answering machine is because there is no more tape left."

"Where were you, Jon? I suppose that you were in Collingwood."

"Mostly. Problem?"

"Oh, nothing that you would be concerned about. I had to pay out a fortune for something that you said that you can fix."

"How was it fixed?"

"Something had to be replaced."

"Something inside the hot water tank?"

"Exactly."

"Which would be illegal for me to do. Any other problems?"

"The garden is a mess …"

"Which is not beyond your abilities to attend to."

"Jon, you have no idea what it's like to manage this house all by myself, especially for someone who's as old as I am."

"So hire somebody."

"That's far too expensive, Jon."

"Then, Mother, you should make plans to move into a retirement village."

"Why do you keep mentioning a retirement village?"

"I think that it's only the second time. Mother, the third school term starts tomorrow, and I need to get myself ready for it. Now if there's nothing else …"

"No, Jon. There's nothing." Andrea hanged up.

Jon tried to call James, but the line beed busy. By the time that Jon beed ready for bed, the line beed still busy.

"Another new term and yet another vice principal," Jeff Bartrum sayed at the staff meeting. "Four so far, and we're only half way through the year. I believe that we've set a record here. Mark, is there anything that you have to say?"

Mark shaked his head.

"Okay, let me introduce Gwen Baretti. She's taking over Mark's classes after teaching at Djawerri High for ... How long?"

"Sixteen years," she replied.

"Welcome to Hidey High, Gwen. And we also have a replacement for Maurice who has decided to go to Korea. Rick Norwood comes to us from teachers college. Rick, can you stand and show yourself? Thank you. Right, let's get to it, everyone."

On the Wednesday, Jon getted home and seed that three messages haved beed recorded on the answering machine during the day.

Instead of calling Melbourne, he called Perth. "I'm going to have to get my number changed, James. Our loving mother is calling me at least three times a night, and I have too much work to do."

"Well, don't pick up."

"That's easier said than done. Listen, I think that she would be far better off in a retirement village than in that old house."

"I agree with you."

"But she won't listen."

"I know."

"James, that house needs a lot of maintenance which I don't have the time, the tools, or the skills to do. And in the case of electrical work, I'm not qualified."

"I know."

"So there's no point for me to go to Melbourne."

"Not until she decides to go into a retirement village. Then you can help with the packing."

"It will have to be during school holidays. Anyway, as you are handling her will, you may like to set some money aside for a unit in a retirement village."

"Of course. Anything else?"

"I'll let you know my new number as soon as I have it."

"Jon, you be looking a bit tired," Ingrid sayed the next day. "Be you okay?"

"I will be when I get my phone number changed," he replied.

"Your mother?"

"Right."

"Take it off the hook."

"Ingrid, what's the point of having a phone if no one can contact me?"

"Haven't you getted an answering machine?"

"Yes, but she doesn't leave messages. She just keeps screaming into the phone."

"Turn down the volume."

"The point is that no one can contact me when she's on the line."

"Yes, I see the problem. Jon, what if she find out your new number?"

"I suppose that it's possible."

"Would you be interested in moving in with me and my son Langton?"

"I … Really?"

"I would have to talk with him first, but I be sure that he would like the idea."

"Well, it's a lovely offer, Ingrid. Can I think about it?"

"Of course. Let me know if and when you be ready."

"Mother, I have an awful lot of work to do, and I really need to get on with it," Jon sayed that evening.

"Before you do, Jon …"

Jon hanged up, taked the phone off the hook, and turned off the answering machine.

"What did Langton say?" Jon asked Ingrid the next day.

"Langton would be delighted. So would you like to move in?"

"Absolutely. Is tomorrow too early?"

"Saturday. That be perfect, Jon. Langton be turning 21 tomorrow, and he have invited his university friends for a party in the evening. He would love you to be there."

"Thank you so much. Let me pay at least part of the rent."

"Oh, don't be silly. Pay the electricity, gas, water, and phone bills, and we be even."

"What's going on, James?" Andrea demanded the following week. "Has Jon changed his number?"

"Not exactly."

"What do you mean: not exactly? Either he has or he hasn't."

"He has moved in with another teacher."

"A male, I suppose."

"Female."

"Oh, well. Things are looking up. Do you have a number?"

"Yes. You just called me on it."

"Oh, you're as bad as Jon. I mean: do you have Jon's new number?"

"Mother, the lady that he has moved in with doesn't want you to have the number."

"Oh, for crying out loud. All right, I'll look it up. What's the name and address?"

"I don't know. Jon didn't tell me."

"Jon, I'm nearly there with getting our mother into a retirement village by the end of this year," James sayed a few weeks more late. "What it will take is for you to be there during your next holidays to help her decide what goes with her and what gets sold. You might like to start with the car. Ever since she ran into another car in a shopping center car park and refused to exchange names and addresses, she is no longer allowed to drive."

"I don't suppose that you can be there."

"Not a chance, Jon. Not with summer coming up. And you'll need to be there during the summer break also to do the final packing, to help her move, and to prepare the house for sale. I'll handle all the paper work from here. Okay?"

"Yeah, sure."

14

"You're not selling the car, Jon," Andrea sayed when Jon arrived in Melbourne at the start of the next school holidays.

"So what do you plan to do with it, Mother? Turn it into a museum?"

"I need it to get around."

"You're not allowed to drive."

"Did James tell you that?"

"He did. Is he wrong?"

"And you complain about people talking behind your back. Anyway, why the hell haven't I got your address and phone number in Sydney?"

"Because Ingrid and I have a lot of work to do in the evenings, and so does her son who's doing final year university."

"Ingrid. Ingrid who?"

"I'm not telling you. Now, I need to look at the car. Have you decided what else needs to be sold?"

"There's nothing, Jon. I don't even know why you're here."

Jon goed to the phone.

"You're not to call him, Jon. I can't afford it."

"Afford what? 008 is a free-call number. Tell you what. I'll pay twice the cost of the call. Okay?"

"Well, I hope that you do."

"Put her on the phone," James sayed after a while. "Listen, Mother dear, I thought that, in the million calls that you've made at my expense, we agreed that you no longer have any use for the car."

"I've changed my mind. Now that Jon's here, he can drive me."

"And when he goes back to Sydney?"

"Then I'll find somebody else to do it."

"Right, Mother. Let it sit in the garage and go down in value to the point where it's not worth selling. Now, how about letting Jon know what's to be sold?"

"There's nothing to be sold."

"Mother, the unit that I've lined up for you is about half the size of the house that you're in now. Now I know that mathematics is not one of your strong points, but do you really think that what you've got in the house can all fit into the unit?"

"No, James, I don't."

"Good. Now we're getting somewhere."

"No, we're not. I'm not going anywhere, James. I'm staying here."

"Oh, that's great. Put Jon back on the phone."

As she handed the phone to Jon: "This call is costing a fortune."

"I said that I'll pay for it, Mother," Jon sayed. "Yes, James."

"I suppose that you've got an idea of what's going on," James sayed.

"I've got a good idea of what's not going on."

"So, what do you want to do? Besides shoot her, I mean."

"I think that a rope tied in exactly the right position would be better."

"What are you two talking about?" Andrea asked.

"We're thinking of moving the house closer to the street."

"You are stupid, Jon. There's no doubt about it."

"You're right, Mother."

"You're not the only one," James sayed. "It will be interesting to see if I will be able to get any part of the deposit back on the unit. So, what are you going to do?"

"I'll stay with friends in Collingwood."

"Oh, it's friends now. Would you mind giving me the number?"

"Indeed, yes."

"Okay, what is it?"

"James, knowing how my loving family feels about my friends, I do mind giving you the number. I'll call you every now and then."

15

"How was Melbourne, Jon?" Ingrid asked when Jon getted back.

"Same as usual: wind, rain, and not a lot of sun."

"Jon, what happened down there? I don't think that the weather down there is the problem. Do you want to talk about it?"

"Let me sum it up in one word: family."

"Okay, you must be hungry. Let me heat something up for you."

As Jon beed eating, he telled Ingrid and Langton much the same as he haved telled Brent and Jody.

"You know, Jon, you're not the only one with family problems," Ingrid sayed when Jon haved finished the meal and the story.

"I know. It seems that everyone has them – some worse than others. Ingrid, when we first met, you said that one of the reasons why you left Zimbabwe is because you had problems with your family and your husbands' families. How many husbands have you had?"

"Only two. Not at the same time, of course. Jon, I really don't want to talk about them. Okay?"

"Fair enough. Will you ever go back to Zimbabwe?"

"Never."

"What about you, Langton?"

"No way. It's easier for me to get a job in Australia," he replied.

"You're in your final year of computer science, right?"

"Yeah, right."

"Have you started applying for jobs yet?"

"Sure. And I really want to get into a company that's developing talking computers. Maybe the way that Mum talks when she's at school can be used to make the programming of them much easier."

In the second week of the last term, Jeff asked Jon to come to his office, and to close the three doors. "Jon, what are your plans for next year?"

"I'm not sure, Jeff. I wouldn't mind getting a permanent position."

"There's no way, Jon. Even if permanent positions were available, you couldn't get one because you quit before. Not only that, there continues to be too many English teachers across the state and across Australia." He paused. "Jon, I am not able to offer you a contract for next year. I wish that I could but it's not possible."

"I understand, Jeff. Thanks for the opportunity to teach this year."

"Thank you for all that you're doing. You will be greatly missed next year. Are you still thinking about Korea?"

"Yes, but I need to talk to Mark about it." Jon goed to Mark's office.

"Sit down, Jon."

"I won't be back here next year, Mark."

"Yes, I know. Jeff told me ten minutes ago. Are you okay?"

"Yeah, I'm okay. I'm lucky to have been offered a contract this year. I don't know whether to thank Hoare or YeongTae for that."

"Jon, did Jeff tell you why your contract won't be extended?"

"Yeah. Because I quit before."

"That's only part of it. Maurice Hoare did a midnight run last week, and he will be back here next year."

"A midnight run?"

"He packed his things, collected his pay, and went straight out to the airport."

"And he will be taking my place?"

"I'm afraid so."

"Even though he quit."

"He didn't quit, Jon. He was given leave without pay until the end of this year. That's something else that Jeff told me ten minutes ago. Look, Jon, I'm not supposed to have told you, so I would really appreciate it if you don't tell anyone else. At least not until the end of the year."

"I won't. I'm glad that you told me though."

"Well, you have every right to know. So, are you still interested in Korea?"

"Sure. But not in a private school."

"No, of course not. Tonight, I'll call my American friend in Seoul and see what he has for next year. I'm sure that he'll have something for you."

"Good evening, Travis. Mark Kang in Sydney. Are you free to talk?"

"Mark! Long time. How are you doing down there?"

"I'm fine; looking forward to the summer break."

"Enjoy it, Mark."

"I don't suppose that you're looking forward to winter."

"You know that I hate the winters here, even though I come from Wisconsin. Anyway, what's up?"

"I have a young guy here who's interested in teaching in Korea next year. Would you have a place for him?"

"Maybe."

"What do you mean: maybe?"

"Well, we've just had an Australian here who the students couldn't understand. What's this guy like?"

"I'm sure that your students will be able to understand him quite easily."

"Is he with you now?"

"No. Do you want to do a phone interview?"

"Well, after this other guy, that's what we do now. What's your time there?"

"We're two hours ahead of you. Would you like to call him at the school tomorrow during our morning break?"

"Sure."

Mark then gived Travis the details. "Listen, can I ask about this other Australian?"

"Well, he only lasted about four months before he did a midnight run. He got into a fight at a pub, waited for his pay, and headed to the airport. He did us a favor; it saved us the trouble of firing him."

"Why did you want to fire him?"

"Well, as I said, the students couldn't understand him. Not only that, he wasn't popular with anyone around here, and he was always complaining."

"And because of that, you wanted to fire him?"

"No, not that. There's a time when he was moving around the female students' housing block in the early morning. The guards reported it."

"Maurice?"

"Oh, you know him?"

"Yes. Maurice Hoare, right?"

"Yeah, right. Did you recommend us to him?"

"No way. I think that he found you through your newspaper advertisements. Travis, the guards who reported it: how did Maurice get past them?"

"That's the question that I've been asking."

"Have you got an answer yet?"

"Not yet. Anyway, it doesn't matter anymore."

"Doesn't it? It sounds to me as though Maurice was set up."

"Are you concerned for him?"

"No, not for Maurice. I'm concerned for Jon."

"What do you mean?"

"I mean that Jon could be set up."

"You're assuming that it's a set-up."

"Travis, what evidence do you have that Maurice was actually in there – aside from what the guards say? Listen, before you have a phone interview with Jon, I want to talk with Maurice. I'll let you know when to call."

"That's tough, Jon," Ingrid sayed that evening. "The kids really like you, and you're well respected by the staff. Anyway, what's your plan now?"

"It looks like Korea, doesn't it? What other choice is there?"

"Thanks for coming in, Maurice," Mark sayed the next day. "Before we talk about next year, would you like to tell me about Korea?"

"What do you want to know?"

"Why you're not there now. Apparently, you only did four months of a one-year contract."

"Mark, I really don't want to talk about it."

"Well, I do because Jon is now interested in going to Korea – to the same university. Listen, I was talking with Travis last night, and he told me that you were reported to have been moving around the female students' housing block in the early hours of the morning."

"And you believe it."

"I don't, mainly because the ones who reported it are supposed to have prevented it. Did you leave Korea because of that, or was it because of the fight in the bar?"

"What else did Travis tell you?"

"That students couldn't understand you, that you weren't popular with anyone, and that you were always complaining."

"There's plenty to complain about there, and from what I can see, there's plenty to complain about at other universities – certainly the private ones. They're only interested in making money, and so their aim is to keep students happy. If a student fails English in their final year, they have an interview with a first-language speaker and a Korean professor where the first-language speaker asks a question and the Korean professor translates it into Korean. And guess what, they all pass."

"That could be because they cannot get a job without a pass in English. What else did you complain about?"

"One of my classes being split where I had 50 students and the other had 15 students, schedules being changed during the term, having classes canceled because there was a three-day holiday in the week, and then being given five days' notice that I had to do make-up classes the following Saturday …"

"Did you do them?"

"No. I had already made plans for that day, and I had no intention of changing them. Mark, I was available on the day that they were scheduled."

"What are your other complaints, Maurice?"

"The attitudes of the students, the attitudes of the other teachers, especially the Americans …"

"Okay, thank you, Maurice. You have been quite helpful."

"I could tell you a lot more."

"I'm sure that you could, but you've told me enough already to realize that you've just had a valuable learning experience."

"What do you mean?"

"Think about it, Maurice. How much of the trouble that you had in Korea was caused by you? And in this school, who won the power struggle with YeongTae Kim?"

"That's because everyone was on his side."

"It's always everyone else who's to blame – never you. There's a reason why everyone was on his side."

"And what's the reason?"

"If I told you, you would just tell me that I'm wrong and give it no more thought. Think about it, Maurice, and be honest. By the way, what was the fight in the bar about?"

"I don't want to talk about it."

"Was it with a Korean or an American?"

"An American. Why?"

"Did he throw the first punch?"

"Yes, he did."

"Could it be because of something that you said to him? Think about it, Maurice."

"Is that all?"

"Not quite. You had an easy ride when Tim Atherton, Neil Drummond, Betty Willis, and Richard Tremayne occupied this chair. That won't be the case with me."

More late in the day, "Jon, there's something that I didn't tell you yesterday," Mark sayed. "Maurice was at the same university that Travis is at, and I'm still not clear as to why Maurice did the midnight run because he had quite a few problems there. After speaking with Travis last night and with Maurice this morning, it's pretty obvious that most of them are due to Maurice – but not all of them."

"I saw Maurice going into your office."

"I hope that you didn't say anything to him."

"I didn't."

"Good. Anyway, Travis wants to call you today for a phone interview, but I want to tell you a few things first." Mark goed on to talk about what was supposed to have happened in the female students' housing block. "As far as I can see, it was a set-up, and what you need to consider is: if that happened to Maurice, then could it happen to anyone else? Something that you could ask Travis is if you have to share housing. From what I've heard, sharing a house or apartment with someone that you've never met before is rarely a comfortable situation."

"It sounds like you're trying to put me off going to Korea."

"I'm telling you what I've just heard."

"Mark, is it possible to have a career in Korea?"

"A career in Korea: interesting expression, but it's not realistic. As far as I know, there's nowhere in Korea which guarantees job satisfaction, or where you can make a career."

"So why did you recommend Korea before?"

"Because I didn't know you well. I've since come to realize that you are more professional than most of the other foreign teachers in Korea, and it may be difficult for you to lower your standards. If you can, then you don't have to restrict yourself to Korea. Japan and Taiwan pay well, and there are other Asian countries where the cost of living is really low. If you can't lower your standards, then you may have to look for something else in Australia."

Just then, the phone ringed.

"It's for you." Mark handed over the phone.

"It's Jenny. Jon, I've got your mother on the line, and she really wants to talk to you. Can I put her through?"

Jon looked at Mark. "It's my mother."

"You can take it here," Mark replied. "No problem."

"Are you sure?"

"Sure. Talk to her."

"Put her through, Jenny. Mother?"

"You haven't called for a while, Jon."

"Sorry, but what is there to talk about?"

"Are you still thinking of going to Korea?"

"I might have to. My contract is not going to be extended."

"What? Aren't you good enough?"

"That's not the reason."

"Then what is the reason?"

"There seems to be more English teachers available than positions to be filled."

"Jon, you have a position now, don't you?"

"Yes, I do."

"Then why are you going to be replaced?"

"It's complicated, Mother. You wouldn't understand."

"Which means that you're not good enough."

"All right, I'm not good enough, even though I'm much better than the teacher who's replacing me."

"So you're just going to rush off to Korea and leave me here alone, are you? Do you have any idea what it's like to be stuck in a big house by myself, and having to hire people to do the jobs that you could do for me?"

"Not really."

"Well, don't you think that you should make an attempt to find out?"

"Why? Mother, it's your choice to stay in that house. James had a unit in a retirement village lined up for you, but you turned it down. If you think that I'm going to move down to Melbourne and stay with you, and do all the jobs around the house that are not illegal for me to do, then you have another think coming. Now, is there anything else?"

"All right, Jon. Forget about me. And forget about getting anything from my will when I die."

"Oh, fine. You can forget about calling me at the school again." Jon hanged up.

"It sounds like relations between you and your mother are not exactly good," Mark sayed.

"Whatever led you to that conclusion, Mark?"

"Oh, just a guess. Jon, if there's anything that I can do to help you get a job, please don't hesitate to let me know Okay?"

"Any jobs in Perth, James?"

"It depends what you're looking for."

"What have you got?"

"Me? What have I got? Nothing, Jon. I keep my staff happy, and they keep me happy. No one is planning to quit. Sorry, I can't help you."

"Perhaps I could be your representative in Sydney. Or Melbourne. Or anywhere."

"Jon, what do you know about fashion design?"

"About as much as you when you first started."

"Jon, I shared a bedroom with you for more than ten years, and there is nothing from that time that suggests that you have a passion for fashion – if you'll excuse the expression. Can you see my point?"

"James, I was twelve when you left home."

"Jon, I don't have any plans to open offices in Sydney, Melbourne, Kurropnagroopna, or anywhere else. If you're quitting teaching again, find something that you're good at."

"James, I am good at teaching. It's not my choice to leave it this time."

"Whatever."

"What are you looking for, Jon?" Brent asked.

"Anything."

"Don't say that. You'll find yourself digging in mines."

"That's it! They're screaming for mine workers in the west."

"It's a tough life over there: hard work, long hours, isolated area, no social life …"

"And plenty of money."

"What's the point of having money if you can't enjoy it? Teaching abroad cannot be all bad or else no one would do it, right? If this Mark guy can find you a good position in Korea, why not take it?"

"To be honest, Brent, I think that I prefer to be working with Jody in the soft drink factory."

By early December, Jon had getted tired of responding to newspaper advertisements only to be telled that he beed either too qualified or qualified in the wrong subject areas. He haved just about decided to tell Mark to ask Travis to call him for the phone interview when there beed a knock at his office door. "YeongTae and Hisham, come in. What can I do for you?"

"It be what we can do for you, sir," YeongTae sayed.

Just then, the phone ringed. "Jon, your mother wants to speak with you," Jenny sayed. "I've been telling her that you're busy when she called before, but I think that you should take this call."

"Thanks, Jenny. Put her through. Sorry, guys. I'll make this quick. Good morning, Mother. I'm with two students right now, so this has to be quick."

"Jon, I've decided to move into the retirement village."

"Good! When?"

"Next month. So I need your help."

"Fine. I'll be there on Christmas Day for the packing."

"I'll need your help with the moving as well."

"Let's discuss that when I'm there. And please don't call the school again." Jon hanged up. "Sorry, guys. You said that you can do something for me?"

"My father owns a printing and publications business," Hisham sayed, "and he wants to talk with you."

"About what?"

"He wants to give you a job."

"I'm sorry that you won't be at Hidey High next year," Omar Moussa sayed as he taked off his glasses. "But if you come and work here, I doubt that I'll still be sorry. Hisham tells me that you are the best teacher that he has ever had, and that tells me that you have passion and commitment. I really need that."

Jon looked around the office. "What would I be doing?"

"How does being the editor of educational books sound?"

"The editor?"

"We're about to branch out into that area. We've done the research, and it shows a lot of promise."

"What if it doesn't work out?"

"Well, I'm sure that we can still find you somewhere in the company to work. Anyway, you need time to think about it, but I need a decision soon. Really soon. Have a look at the job details and the salary, and get back to me. Tomorrow if you can."

"Oh, no. Not tomorrow."

"How long do you need?"

"About two seconds. The answer is yes."

16

When Andrea opened the front door, a dog comed out and pressed itself into Jon's leg. Jon reached down and stroked it a few times before going into the house.

"Where did you get it?" he asked.

"From the lost dogs home."

The dog beed giving more attention to Jon. "What's the dog's name?"

"Her name is Josie."

"Josie. Where did you get that god-awful name?"

The dog goed to Jon and sitted in front of him, and he gived it a few more strokes.

"I named it after your father, Jon."

"Oh, I see. It's a nice dog. How often do you … How often do you take it out for exercise?"

"Whenever I can."

"How often is that?"

"Two or three times a week."

"Has it been out today?"

"No, Jon. I haven't had time today."

"Hey, Josie. Would you like to go …"

Now Jon haved the dog's complete attention.

"… for a walk?"

The dog immediately runned to where its lead beed hanging. Jon goed over and taked the lead down and attached it to its collar.

"What have you decided, Mother?"

"About what?"

"About what goes to the retirement village and what gets sold."

"It's all going to the retirement village."

"It is? Then I need to have a look at the plan of the unit when I come back."

"Why?"

"Because I need to see it."

"I don't see why. Are you going to do the packing or not?"

"I'll start packing after I see the plan. I also want the car keys."

"What do you want them for?"

"To stick in a power point and turn myself into a Christmas tree."

"Jon, you're not funny. What do you want the car keys for?"

"Just have the plan of the unit and the car keys ready for when I get back. And the garage key."

As he leaded the dog into a nearby park, Jon seed notices that sayed that dogs need to be keeped on their leads, and any of their droppings need to be picked up and taked away. He looked around, seed no one in the park, hesitated, and letted the dog off the lead. The dog runned around smelling grass and the bases of trees before making a fresh deposit. Jon goed to a trash can, picked out a few food wrappings, goed over to the warm deposit, and carefully picked it up.

"Josie!"

To Jon's relief, the dog immediately stopped smelling a tree and runned to him. With the dog running beside him, Jon runned up to the trash can, dropped the wrappings with the warm deposit into it, and runned toward the small stream. Jon stopped at the bank; the dog doedn't.

"What took you so long?" Andrea asked when they returned. "And look at the dog! It's all wet. Take it around the back; it's not coming into the house like that. You do realize that you're not supposed to let a dog off the lead in a public place. And what did you do with its droppings?"

"I put them in the trash can."

"Oh, for crying out loud, Jon. You're not supposed to do that."

"Mother, I didn't know. You could have given me something for its droppings before I left."

When Jon leaded the dog around the back, he seed that, unlike the front, the grass havedn't beed cutted for a while, and a more close look revealed that among the long grass, there beed a large number of deposits, now cool and some with a type of hair coming out of some of them.

"I need the garage key and the car keys, Mother," Jon sayed when he goed back inside.

"I can't find the car keys, Jon."

"Then just give me the garage key."

"You're not going to try and break into the car, are you?"

"No, I'm not."

"Then why do you want to go into the garage?"

"The yard at the back needs a lot of attention. Now why is that?"

"I need to save money, Jon."

"Interesting. Key? I'll look at the plan of the unit when I've finished."

"I can't find it, Jon."

"Then keep looking."

After an hour and a shower, "Jon, I can't find the plan. Just start the packing. I'm moving on Monday the fourth."

"Okay, I'll let you sort things out with the moving guys. I won't be here."

"What do you mean: you won't be here?"

"I start my new job that day."

"Can't you delay it?"

"Oh, great idea. New job, and I call in sick before I even start it. Do you have any more brilliant ideas like that? Right, I'll start on the kitchen things."

"Moving day is going to be a disaster," Jon telled James when Andrea goed under the shower. "The dear sweet one thinks that everything in the house will go into the unit. I asked for the plan of the unit but she cannot seem to find it. James, you know that I have to be back in Sydney on the third."

"Yes, you told me, and I'm glad that you found a job. I suppose that the car is still there."

"It is. She cannot find the car keys either."

"Then find them, Jon, and get rid of the bloody thing. I don't care what you do with it. Dump it if you have to. I want that house completely empty at the end of moving day. I'll tell the moving guys to get as much as they can into the unit and the garage, leave the rest outside, and then leave. It's just as well that neither of us will be there to see the drama."

Not only beed the plan of the retirement unit on the study desk, but the car keys beed in the top drawer.

Out in the garage, Jon beed not surprised when the engine failed to turn over.

"Where are you sleeping tonight?" Brent asked when Jon called him.

"On my back and sides."

"Are you sleeping there or here?"

"With all the extra work to be done, I have to sleep here, Brent. Listen, the reason that I'm calling is that I need help with my mother's car."

"Oh, I'm not good with cars, Jon. That's one reason why I haven't got one. Hey, Jody. What are you like with cars?"

"Pretty good," comed from a distance.

"Here. Talk with Jon."

"Hello?"

"Jody. What days don't you work?"

"I've got Monday and Tuesday off next week. Why?"

The next morning, Andrea standed and watched Jon doing the packing. "That's not the way that your father would have done it," she sayed after a while.

"What's wrong with the way that I'm doing it? Unless the boxes are handled really roughly, there's no way that anything's going to break."

"How can I be sure of that?"

"Okay, Mother, let's take them to the unit next week. Okay?"

"Well, now you're finally showing some common sense."

"Thank you very much. By the way, I have a friend coming here next week to look at the car."

"There's no way that I can get it started," Jody sayed the following Tuesday.

"Can we roll-start it?" Jon asked.

"It's an automatic. No way. The only way to get it started is to use the power in your car. Do you have the leads?"

"I do. Let me bring my car in."

While they beed doing it, Andrea comed out. "I hope that you know what you're doing. This is a valuable car."

Jody laughed. "Mrs. Mamjjasond, the only people who would find any value in this car are spare parts dealers."

"Is that right? By the way, how did you get to know my son?"

"He was one of my students last year, Mother," Jon sayed.

"In Kurropnagroopna."

"That's right, Mother. Where else?"

"What's your name?"

"I'm Jody Greggs."

"Jodie? Are you a female?"

"No, ma'am. The last time that I looked, I'm definitely a male."

"All right, Mother," Jon sayed. "Back inside and let us get on with the job. Go, Mother. Go. Go!"

"You have some explaining to do," she sayed as she goed back inside.

"Are you serious, Jody? This car is only good for spare parts?"

"Jon, this car will die on the road within a week. There's a spare parts place next to where I work, and I know the owner. Let's take it there in the morning. I'll help you with the packing for the rest of the day when we get this thing started."

After fifteen minutes, "We both need a shower, Mother," Jon sayed.

"I suppose that you do," she replied. "I hope that you're not intending to shower together."

"Right, that's it. Let's go, Jody."

"What? You're leaving?"

"Mother, I cannot control your mind or your mouth, and I doubt that you can either. All the best with the move."

"So you're just going to walk out on me; abandon me when I really need you. If you walk out that door, don't bother coming back. And don't expect to get anything from my will either."

"You made that clear before, Mother."

"Then why are you here?"

"I came to help you, but if you're giving all your money to James, then perhaps he should do more to earn it. Come on, Jody. Let's get out of here."

Neither Jon nor Jody could think of anything to say as they left. Eventually, "I'm sorry that you had to see that," Jon sayed. "I should have known that something like that was going to happen. I should have bloody known."

"So what are you going to do now?"

"What I'm not going to do is anything more for that woman. She can find someone else to get rid of that car when she realizes that it has to be got rid of."

"What about the packing?"

"Most of it has been done; the rest can be handled by the moving guys. I'm already feeling sorry for them."

"When are you going back to Sydney?"

"On the second – as planned. Jody, I want to see in the new year with you and Brent and all of your friends, and I want the chance to recover on New Year's Day. When I get a vacation, I want to come to Melbourne, but only to see you and Brent. Not that bloody woman. I never want to see her again. Ever."

"Will you ever visit Kurropnagroopna again?"

"It's possible."

"Good luck with the new job. I really hope that it works out for you."

"So do I. And I hope that things keep going well for you at the soft drink factory."

"Can I give you a piece of advice? If you don't mind."

"I hope that it's not something like 'Go back and help your mother.'"

"No, I wouldn't dare suggest that."

"Then what?"

"Jon, I know that you got to know Brent and my cousin by picking them up from the side of the road ..."

"Yes, and YeongTae Kim, which led to a teaching job at Hidey High, which in turn has led to this new job that starts on Monday. Let me guess. You're about to suggest that I've been lucky, and that I shouldn't pick up any more strangers."

"That's exactly right."

"You know, you're not the first to say that."

"I didn't say it. You didn't give me the chance to say it. Anyway, it's your choice, Jon."

"Indeed it is, Jody. And the advice is good. Thank you."

As Jody wondered how long he would stay in the soft drink factory, Jon beed thinking about the printing and publications business, wondering if Hisham could become his boss, and if YeongTae would get a job there writing with simple English rather than standard English.

AUTHOR'S NOTE

The primary aim of this novel is to demonstrate the practicality of the English that Ingrid MacElvers used at school, and which YeongTae chose to adopt. Here, there are no exceptions to the basic rules of grammar, and this allows the choices of having:

be instead of *am*, *is*, and *are*;

have instead of *has*;

no addition of *s* or *es* to other verbs;

beed instead of *was*, *were*, and *been*;

all past participles and active past simple verbs ending in *ed*;

all singular nouns adding *s* or *es* to form the plural;

and no adjectives and adverbs adding *er*, *e*, *est*, or *st* to form comparatives.

The secondary aim of this novel is to use only words that appear within the top 90% of everyday English, and for this purpose, a list of 2700 was compiled and can be found in the book *Intish: Introductory and International English* by David Kent. In this novel, 1404 (52%) of these words are used with endings for noun plurals, verb tenses and participles, and comparative adjectives and adverbs, plus names, titles, numbers, and interjections. Here are the 1404 words:

a, abandon, ability, able, about, above, abroad, absence, absolutely, abuse, accept, access, accident, accuse, achieve, achievement, acknowledge, across, act, action, activity, actually, adapt, add, address, administration, administrative, advantage, advertisement, advice, advise, affair, affect, afford, afraid, after, afternoon, again, against, age, ago, agree, agreement, ahead, aim, air, airport, alcohol, alive, all, allow, almost, alone, along, already, also, although, always, among, amount, an, and, angry, animal, announce, another, answer, any, anymore, anyone, anything, anyway, anywhere, apartment, apologize, apparently, appear, appearance, apply, appoint, appreciate, approach, approve, area, argue, argument, arm, around, arrange, arrangement, arrest, arrive, as, aside, ask, asleep, assume, at, atmosphere, attach, attempt, attend, attention, attitude, author, automatic, available, avoid, aware, away, awful,

back, bad, badly, bag, bank, bar, base, basic, basically, basis, bathroom, be, beautiful, beauty, because, become, bed, bedroom, before, behave, behavior, behind, being, belief, believe, bell, belong, below, bend, benefit, beside, besides, better, between, beyond, big, bike, bill, bit, bite, black, blame, blind, block, blood, bloody, blue, board, body, book, bore, boring, boss, both, bother, box, boy, branch, bread, break, breakfast, breath, breathe, brick, bridge, brief, briefly, bright, brilliant, bring, broad, brother, brown, brush, budget, bug, burn, bus, business, busy, but, button, by,

call, can, cancel, car, card, care, career, careful, carefully, carry, case, catch, category, cause, cell, center, centimeter, central, certainly, chair, chance, change, chapter, character, charge, chart, check, chest, chicken, child, childhood, choice, choose, church, circle, circumstance, city, claim, class, classroom, clean, clear, clearly, climate, climb, close, closed, clothes, cloud, coat, coffee, cold, collapse, collar, collect, college, color, combine, come, comfortable, command, comment, commitment, common, communicate, communication, company, complain, complaint, complete, completely, complicated, computer, concern, concerned, conclude, conclusion, conference, confident, conflict, confuse, consider, contact, continue, contract, control, conversation, convince, cook, cool, copy, corner, correct, cost, could, count, country, couple, course, cousin, cover, crazy, create, creative, crime, criminal, critical, cross, crowd, cry, cup, cut, cute, dad, dance, dare, dark, date, day, dead, deal, dealer, dear, debt, decide, decision, deep, defend, definitely, degree, delay, delight, demand, deny, department, depend, deposit, depression, deserve, design, desk, despite, destroy, detail, develop, development, die, difference, different, difficult, dig, dinner, director, dirt, disappear, disappointed, disaster, discipline, discuss, disease, distance, district, disturb, divide, do, doctor, dog, door, double, doubt, down, dozen, drag, drama, drawer, dream, dress, drink, drive, driver, drop, drug, drunk, due, dump, during, dust, duty,

each, ear, early, earn, ease, easily, east, easy, eat, editor, education, educational, effective, effectively, egg, either, electrical, electricity, elevator, else, embarrassed, emotional, empty, encourage, end, engine, enjoy, enough, enter, enthusiasm, entry, environment, equal, equally, escape, especially, essay, even, evening, eventually, ever, every, everyone, everything, evidence, exact, exactly, exam, example, excellent, except, exception, exchange, excuse, exercise, exist, expect, expense, expensive, experience, experienced, explain, express, expression, extend, extra, extremely, eye,

face, fact, factory, fail, fair, fairly, fall, familiar, family, far, fashion, fast, father, favor, favorite, feel, feeling, female, few, field, fight, figure, file, fill, final, finally, find, fine, finish, fire, first, fit, fix, fixed, flight, floor, fly, focus, follow, following, food, foot, football, for, force, foreign, forget, form, former, fortune, forward, free, freedom, fresh, friend, friendly, from, front, full, funeral, funny, furniture, further, future,

game, garage, garden, gas, gather, gay, generation, gentleman, gently, get, girlfriend, give, glad, glass, go, goal, god, good, government, grade, graduate, grand, grandfather, grandmother, grass, gray, great, greatly, green, ground, group, guarantee, guard, guess, guy, habit, hair, half, hand, handle, hang, happen, happy, hard, hardly, hate, have, he, head, health, healthy, hear, heat, heavily, heavy, hell, hello, help, helpful, her, here, herself, hesitate, hi, high, highly, highway, him, himself, hire, his, history, hit, hold, holiday, home, homework, honest, hook, hope, horror, horse, hospital, hot, hotel, hour, house, housing, how, however, human, hungry, hunt, husband,

I, idea, if, ignore, ill, illegal, illness, imagination, imagine, immediately, important, impose, impression, in, incident, include, including, indeed, inform, information, inside, insist, instead, instruction, insurance, intelligence, intelligent, intend, intention, interest, interested, interesting, interview, into, introduce, invite, isolate, issue, it, its, itself,

jacket, job, join, joke, journey, judge, jump, just, justify,

keep, key, kick, kid, kill, kilometer, kind, kitchen, knock, know,

label, labor, ladder, lady, land, language, large, last, late, latter, laugh, lead, league, lean, learn, least, leave, left, leg, legal, less, lesson, let, level, library, license, lie, life, lift, light, like, likely, limit, limited, line, list, listen, literature, little, live, living, local, lock, long, look, loose, lose, losed, lot, loud, love, lovely, low, lower, luck, lucky, lunch,

machine, magazine, main, mainly, maintenance, make, male, man, manage, many, march, mark, marriage, married, marry, mate, math (in Australia: *maths*), *mathematics, matter, may, maybe, me, meal, mean, medical, meet, meeting, mention, mess, message, metal, middle, midnight, might, milk, mind, mine, minute, miss, mission, mistake, mix, mobile, mom* (in Australia: *mum*), *moment, money, month, more, morning, most, mostly, mother, mountain, mouse, mouth, move, movie, much, mud, museum, must, my, myself, name, native, natural, nature, near, nearby, nearly, necessary, need, negative, neighbor, neighborhood, neither, nerve, never, nevertheless, new, news, newspaper, next, nice, night, no, none, nor, normal, normally, north, not, note, nothing, notice, novel, now, nowhere, number, nurse,*

object, obvious, obviously, occupy, occur, of, off, offer, office, officer, official, often, okay, old, on, once, one, only, onto, open, opinion, opportunity, opposite, or, order, organize, other, otherwise, our, out, outside, over, own, owner,

pack, pain, paint, painting, pair, paper, parent, park, part, partner, party, pass, passage, passenger, passion, past, patient, pause, pay, peace, pen, perfect, performance, perhaps, period, permanent, person, personal, phone, physical, pick, piece, pipe, pizza, place, plan, plane, plate, platform, play, please, pleased, pleasure, plenty, point, police, policy, popular, position, possess, possible, possibly, post, potential, power, practice, prefer, preparation, prepare, present, press, pressure, pretty, prevent, previous, primary, principal, print, priority, private, probably, problem, professional, professor, profit, program, promise, proof, proper, properly, proud, prove, provide, provided, pub, public, publication, pull, punch, purple, purpose, push, put,

qualify, quality, quantity, queen, question, quick, quickly, quiet, quit, quite,

race, radio, rain, raise, rarely, rather, reach, read, reading, ready, real, realistic, reality, realize, really, reason, reasonable, receive, recently, reception, recipe, recommend, recommendation, record, recover, red, reduce, refuse, regard, register, regret, regular, relation, relationship, relief, relieve, religion, religious, remain, remaining, remark, remember, rent, repeat, replace, replacement, reply, report, representative, request, require, research, reserve, respect, respond, response, responsibility, rest, restaurant, restrict, result, retire, retirement, return, reveal, rid, ride, right, ring, rip, rise, risk, road, roll, roof, room, root, rope, roughly, round, rub, ruin, rule, run, rush,

salary, sale, salt, same, sand, sandwich, satisfaction, satisfy, save, say, scene, schedule, scheme, school, science, score, scream, search, seat, second, secretary, secure, see, seem, sell, send, sense, sensitive, sentence, separate, serious, seriously, serve, service, set, settle, several, severe, sex, sexual, shake, shame, share, she, shift, ship, shirt, shoot, shop, shopping, short, should, shoulder, shout, show, shower, sick, side, sign, silence, silly, simple, simply, since, sister, sit, situation, size, skill, sky, sleep, slow, small, smell, smile, smoke, so, social, soft, solution, some, somebody, someone, something, somewhere, son, song, soon, sorry, sort, sound, soup, south, spare, speak, speaker, special, specific, speech, speed, spell, spend, split, square, staff, stage, stand, standard, stare, start, state, station, stay, steak, step, stick, still, stop, store, story, straight, strain, strange, stranger, strategy, stream, street, strength, stress, strike, stroke, strong, structure, struggle, student, study, stupid, style, subject, such, suddenly, suffer, sugar, suggest, suggestion, suit, suitable, sum, summer, sun, support, suppose, sure, surely, surface, surprise, surprised, survive, sweet, switch, sympathy,

table, take, talk, tall, tank, tap, tape, tax, taxi, tea, teach, teacher, teaching, team, tear, television, tell, term, terribly, test, than, thank, thanks, that, the, their, them, then, there, therefore, these, they, thick, thin, thing, think, this, those, though, thought, through, throw, ticket, tie, tight, time, tired, to, today, together, tomorrow, tongue, tonight, too, tool, top, touch, tough, toward, towel, town, trade, traffic, train, transfer, translate, trash, travel, treat, treatment, tree, trip, trouble, truck, true, trust, truth, try, turn, twice, type, ultimately, under, understand, understanding, unfortunately, unique, unit, university, unless, unlike, until, unusual, up, upset, upstairs, urban, us, use, used, useful, usual, usually,

vacation, valuable, value, vegetable, vehicle, very, vice, view, village, violence, visit, voice, volume, vote,

wait, wake, walk, wall, want, warm, warning, wash, waste, watch, water, wave, way, we, weak, wear, weather, week, weekend, weight, welcome, well, west, wet, what, whatever, when, whenever, where, whereas, whether, which, while, white, who, whoever, whole, whose, why, wide, wife, will, willing, win, wind, window, winter, wire, wise, wish, with, withdraw, within, without, woman, wonder, wonderful, wood, word, work, worker, world, worried, worry, worth, would, wrap, write, writer, writing, wrong,

yard, yeah, year, yes, yesterday, yet, you, young, your, yours, yourself.

ABOUT THE AUTHOR

Coming from a teaching background, Noel David is one of many who was attracted to Korea to help fill a demand for first-language speakers of English, and he soon realized that effective communication is more important than grammatical correctness. At intish.com, he has offered choices to speak without any exceptions to the basic rules of grammar, and provided dialogs, stories, jokes, song lyrics, and discussions using all of those choices.

www.ingramcontent.com/pod-product-compliance
Lightning Source LLC
Chambersburg PA
CBHW021105130626
46554CB00002B/536